MURDER AT THE BASEBALL HALL OF FAME

Other Novels by David Daniel

The Skelly Man
The Heaven Stone
The Tuesday Man
Ark

MURDER AT THE BASEBALL HALL OF FAME

DAVID DANIEL
AND
CHRIS CARPENTER

ST. MARTIN'S PRESS ❧ NEW YORK

A THOMAS DUNNE BOOK.
An imprint of St. Martin's Press.

Book design by Scott Levine

Library of Congress Cataloging-in-Publication Data

Daniel, David
    Murder at the Baseball Hall of Fame / David Daniel and
Chris Carpenter. — 1st ed.
       p.   cm.
    "A Thomas Dunne book."
    ISBN 0-312-14683-3 (hardcover)
    I. Carpenter, Chris.   II. Title.
PS3554.A5383M87   1996
813'.54—dc20   96-20200
                                       CIP

10 9 8 7 6 5 4 3 2

To our fathers, who first taught us the game.

With thanks to Beverly McCoy, Patricia Updyke-Thorpe, and Gary Watkins. And to the police in the village of Cooperstown, New York.

We are born to hold
the things of this world to raise dead clay
Incorruptible!
— Jim Provencher

When you come to a fork in the road, take it.
— Yogi Berra

PART ONE

THE PICKOFF

IN THE EARLY AUGUST DUSK A MOTORBOAT PURRED FAR out on Otsego Lake and sent reflections of lights from camps on the opposite shore shimmering in its wake like waterborne comets. On this shore, Chinese lanterns glowed along the perimeters of fresh-cut lawn, and orchestra music drifted from a gazebo at Frank Branco's back. He sipped beer and thought about baseball. And why not? Induction weekend here in Cooperstown at the Baseball Hall of Fame would do that.

But he was thinking about one particular moment in baseball, in a place far from here: a warm, cricket-stitched night a lot of years ago. Frank at seventeen. A special game against Quincy for a league title. A crack of the bat and the ball looping out toward him in right field. Frank moving in to set up for the catch, an easy out to end the game, win the championship. But the lights. High school baseball wasn't a night sport in eastern Massachusetts. The ball vanished in the intense white glare, and for that one instant . . .

"Yo! Hey, Branki—I mean Franco!" whooped a voice.

Frank turned. Tom Webster, radio personality for Utica's WENC and Branco's guide, was stumbling down the sloping lawn.

His present condition had got its start that afternoon at Doubleday Field, with beer in paper cups. Now Webster lifted a martini glass in toast. Tripping, he sloshed the contents onto Frank's sport coat. Webster scarcely seemed to notice. He handed over the glass and clapped Frank's shoulder. "Gemme another drinkie, will ya Branki Frinko. They shumme off. Good fella. Gotta take a leak." And he shuffled to the lake's edge to do so.

Frank watched him a moment to be sure he didn't fall in, then started up the lawn. Frank brushed at his lapel, but he didn't care about the sport coat. Polyester was built for wear. At Doubleday that afternoon, the Phillies had trimmed the Mariners 3–2 in the annual Hall of Fame induction game, and though Frank had been rooting for the American League, he didn't care about that either. This was his first visit to Cooperstown, and he was loving it.

At the outdoor bar Frank asked the barman to fill the martini glass with water and put an olive in it. The orchestra was playing "Joy to the World," the one with Jeremiah the bullfrog, giving it a Latin tempo. Next to him, a tanned woman in a deep-green dress turned to peer at Frank. She looked to be in her mid-forties, his age, and had pale hair that in the glow from the Chinese lanterns seemed spun around her head like cotton candy. Her scent was exotic on the cool night air. Frank squared his shoulders. "Good evening," he said, thinking maybe he would ask her to dance if a slow one came up.

Looking him over carefully, the woman narrowed one eye finally. "Cleveland?"

"Boston," he said.

Slight puzzlement. "You were with the Red Sox?"

"The cops," he said. "I'm private now."

Her look became befuddlement. "Then, I don't understand."

Frank shrugged. It had taken him a while too. Disappointed, he watched her walk off, her dress bright as a new-mown outfield. The bartender acknowledged the exchange. It was an easy mistake to make, he said. "This time of year you could pop a champagne cork and hit an ex-ballplayer. Plenty of names around, sure.

Saw Stan the Man earlier. Bob Feller, Reggie, Joe Morgan, Rollie Fingers, Whitey Ford. Remember Moose Skowron? But a lot of never-weres come up for the weekend too. From Boston I heard you say?"

Frank told it. The trip here for the annual induction weekend had come as the result of a promotion on a Boston radio sports call-in show. A Fan's Fantasy. Be the lucky winner and make your athletic dream come true. "They picked my name out of a cap that Dick Radatz wore. About this big around."

Included in the package had been Tom Webster, his host from a sister station in Utica, whose press pass had given them stage-side access to the induction ceremony, three nights at the Otesaga Hotel, and an invitation to this party. There were parties all over Cooperstown tonight, the select ones held to honor the people anointed this year, and to give Hall of Famers, past and present, a chance to schmooze. None of the Hofers was here, nor were any of the other players the bartender mentioned, but Frank wasn't fussy. And maybe he did look the part of the old ballplayer, some guy who had broken in in the late sixties say, and had hit .225 lifetime. His size and his ropy physique and the all-season tan probably said outfielder. The dent in the bridge of his nose . . . well, who knew? And what the hell, he was having fun. Let folks have their fantasies.

Frank was almost back to the lake's edge, searching the shadowed lawn for Tom Webster, when he heard the snapping and crackling. He turned to see a car crash out of the woods up near the house. It came gunning down across the yard as if it were being chased. It took down a strand of Chinese lanterns which got hooked on the antenna and was pulled along like a scarf of fireflies. The car was headed for the lake, except standing between it and the water was the gazebo, where the orchestra was. There were shouts, then the music quit. Microphones clattered over. Musicians clutching clarinets and guitars against their pink-ruffled shirtfronts leaped from the platform and scrambled in all directions.

The car hit the gazebo, knocking out supports, filling the night with noise and the flying sticks of a marimba, and came to an abrupt and hissing halt.

Way to crash a party, Frank thought. Obeying old habit, he looked at his watch, noting the time. Just past nine. Then he was dropping the drinks and starting toward the wreckage at a jog, trying to ignore the pinch from the old gunshot wound in his left leg.

Taller than most of the party guests already gathered, Frank looked over their heads at the crumpled car. A Plymouth, he saw; not new. He went nearer. Lanterns strewn on the grass threw weird patterns on the car's windows, so it took him a moment to see the driver slumped at the steering wheel. The man's head was turned, and his face peered out the closed window. Someone rapped on the glass and called to him, but he didn't move. There was no one else visible inside. Over the hissing of the motor, Frank heard another sound, like a cough, and suddenly flames sprang from the crunched grille.

"Get back," Frank called, but his voice was only one sound among many. The onlookers merely shifted position. Frank shouldered through. He grabbed the driver's door handle and pulled. The door stayed shut: locked from the inside. Resting one hand on the roof for balance, he raised his foot and kicked the glass of the back-door window. Yeah, right. No effect. He tried again, same result. Flames were licking up from under the sprung hood with quick, bright tongues.

Frank looked around quickly, then pointed. "Microphone!" he shouted. One person seemed to understand. A woman bent into the wreckage of the gazebo and retrieved a metal mike stand. Frank took it, telling the woman, "Call nine-one-one," then swung the heavy base against the rear-door window. The pane bent inward, a brightly stippled net in the firelight. The next time the stand went through it in a burst of glass. Frank reached through and unlocked the driver's door.

As he leaned into the Plymouth, he caught a whiff of a bright, astringent smell. Booze? Was the driver drunk? He tried to identify the smell but couldn't and he let it go. He spoke to the driver. No response. He patted the man's cheek. No movement. He shook the man. Window chips spilled from the man's chest and shoulders. Frank wondered: Was there a middle ground between moving an accident victim too much and not enough? Flames were darting along the rocker panel, feeding with a crackling sound. Frank gripped the driver's shoulders—meaty under the fabric of his Glen plaid blazer—and tugged. But the medical question was academic. The man was pinned by the steering wheel.

Some calmer part of Frank's mind began to operate. He fingered the side of the driver's throat. Feeling for a pulse. Waiting.

"God sakes, run!" somebody yelled behind him.

Frank got his hands under the man's arms and pulled. Something, maybe ribs, made a low grinding. Frank pulled harder, but the man wouldn't budge.

"Run!"

Frank still held the man. He felt heat at his ankles where flames had sprouted from under the car. He stamped at burning grass. He shoved his hand inside the driver's jacket, still looking for a heartbeat—finding instead a wallet in the inner pocket. He drew it out. He could feel the heat on his wrists now and he was thinking: Water last time, fire now, and the result would be the same and there was nothing he could do to change that.

"It's gonna blow!"

The shout jarred Frank's thoughts, and with a lurch of fear he twisted away and followed the party guests scattering across the grass just before the car filled the night with fireworks.

The cruiser came down the lawn at a dignified speed, no blue lights or siren, and stopped forty feet from the smoldering gazebo and the burned-out car. After the explosion, people had finally begun to react. Several had restrung enough lanterns to give some light, while others pulled down a garden hose and held the flames to a standoff until a Cooperstown fire truck arrived with chemical foam. Even so, the car was a hulk of smoking steel and plastic marooned in a circle of scorched grass. Except for the two firefighters, no one had gone close enough yet to see what had become of the driver.

Frank held a chunk of ice first against one wrist, then the other, and watched a policeman climb out of the cruiser. He crossed in front of his still-lit headlamps, and Frank saw he was of medium height and more than medium weight. He had on a pale blue short-sleeve uniform shirt and campaign hat and a Sam Browne belt that was busy with every accessory a cop could have. They jingled and flapped as he came across the lawn with a surprisingly delicate stride, as if the inconsistent light were throwing his depth perception off, making every step deliberate. The host and hostess of the party met him, and together they walked over to where one of the firemen stood, a big red-haired guy with a handlebar mustache. The cop conferred a moment with the fireman, and together they approached the car. The fireman had a battle lantern, which he shone into the wreck. Frank got his first prolonged look then. The steering wheel had melted away and vanished, but that didn't seem to matter to the blackened form of what had been the driver. He still had his arms out; but without the wheel he appeared to be shoving back at a world which had crowded too close. Frank's stomach rolled. Mercifully the fireman shut the light off.

Except for crickets and the low crackle of two-way radios, the night had a kind of benumbed stillness. The smell of wet smoke hung in the cool air. Again the cop spoke with the home owners. The hostess said something to him and pointed in Frank's direction. Frank dropped the chunk of ice on the grass as the cop came over.

"My name's Jim Bolick, chief of police," he said.

Frank murmured his own name.

"Understand you tried to get the victim out."

"Tried," Frank agreed.

"Don't you know moving an accident victim might hurt him more? Or could've."

"With a car getting ready to explode?"

Bolick frowned. "You get burned?"

"Singed a few hairs. I'm okay."

"Come on up and sit in the car a minute. Let's talk."

Frank got into the front seat as Bolick went around and squeezed in under the steering wheel. The cruiser was a lot better kept than the Boston cruisers had been. It smelled of pine woods. Bolick plucked a notepad from one pouch in his belt and a pencil from another and swiveled around to face Frank. His uniform shirt had been crisp once, but it had wilted so that the only part wrinkle-free was the patch stretched tight over his midriff.

"Your name again?" he said.

Frank repeated and spelled it.

"Age?"

"Forty-two."

Bolick went through the boilerplate quickly. He didn't lick the pencil point as he jotted. "Okay, what happened?"

Frank described what he had seen and done. Finally he handed over the victim's wallet. Bolick gave him a questioning look.

"I was on the cops nine years," Frank volunteered.

If Bolick picked up on the use of past tense, he didn't pursue it, or ask any questions. He went through the wallet, using a penlight from his belt. There wasn't much: a little paper, even less cash. He studied the laminated driver's license a moment, then set the wallet aside. Wrinkling his nose, he said, "You been drinking?"

"A couple beers."

"Beers?"

"My coat drank a martini."

Just then red lights splashed the cruiser's interior. Both men turned to see an ambulance coming down the lawn. It wasn't a great night for the grass. "Sit tight," Bolick said, and got out and walked over to confer with a pair of EMTs.

9

Remembering for the first time the odor he had smelled upon leaning into the Plymouth, Frank sniffed his hands. They were clean and cool from holding ice. On the seat where Bolick had left it was the victim's wallet. Frank picked it up. There was a gasoline company credit card, charge slips, a few business cards for tradesmen with Utica addresses, four Elvis postage stamps, a pair of ticket stubs to a Mets game from May, and twelve dollars in cash. Frank had left his reading glasses at the Otesaga Hotel and had to squint in the weak light to read the license. It was issued to a Herbert W. Frawley of Utica, fifty-eight years old Frank calculated from the birth date. As he was putting things back, Frank noticed an inner compartment. He opened it. He tweezed out a square of crisp, yellowed paper. Unfolding it he saw it was a scorecard from a baseball game. Frank tried to make out the names and numbers on it, but the writing was faded.

He looked up at the jingle-flap sounds of Chief Bolick returning. On an impulse Frank refolded the scorecard and palmed it.

"All right, friend," Bolick said, leaning into the cruiser's open window. "That'll do it. Good night."

Herbert Frawley, RF. b. 9/17/35. Lebanon, OH. T-L. B-L.
Six major-league seasons. 1956–61. Four teams.
Lifetime batting avg. .238

IT MADE A SLIM LITTLE ENTRY ON PAGE 871 OF ONE OF THE
fat baseball books Frank had consulted at Augur's bookstore on
Main Street, even when you added the newest stat: deceased.
Frank looked up as a young police officer came to the chest-high
wooden counter. Frank asked if Chief Bolick was in.

"Around here somewhere. You want to see him?"

Frank said yes, and gave his name. The officer went to find
his boss.

Like a lot of the buildings in the village of Cooperstown, the
one housing police headquarters was old, a stately gray stone struc-
ture, with tall white columns, dating from a quaint past century
when, according to legend, Abner Doubleday organized a group
of farm boys in a local pasture and the game of baseball was born.
A half-trying third baseman could have yanked a ball across the

street and put it on the front steps of the National Baseball Hall of Fame, or rolled a liner up to the feet of the statue of James Fenimore Cooper, sitting in the park alongside, musing on what his little village had become.

The office was small, with a duty desk, several steel file cabinets, and the inevitable displays of insignia patches from police organizations around the country. A few wanted posters shared a bulletin board with the department's duty roster.

The young officer returned. "Okay, he'll be with you in a couple minutes, sir. You can wait right there in his office if you like."

"Thanks."

The Chief's office was fresh with the smells of remodeling: new carpet, wallboard, and paint. The name block on the desk said Chief James R. Bolick. On a bookshelf behind the desk, occupying the one corner not filled with procedure manuals and file folders, sat an old riot helmet with a plastic visor. For when baseball fever got too virulent? Frank wondered.

One of the side walls was covered with photographs: James R. Bolick as a trim young man, with a high school sweetheart; in crew cut and army green; at a New York police academy graduation ceremony, class of '83. There were pictures of Bolick with his family, each successive shot revealing another child—four in total, apparently—and more pounds. Pictures with Hank Aaron, Don Drysdale, Brooks Robinson, a batting pose with Pete Rose—both men sporting considerable girth. It was probably as close to the Hall as Rose was likely to get anytime soon, Frank thought. If the chief ever opened a restaurant, all he'd need was food.

Bolick's jingling belt announced him. He stepped into the tiny space and gave an abrupt lift of his chin. "Help you?"

"Just thought I'd touch base," Frank said. The clichés came easy in this town.

"About? . . ."

It came to Frank that Bolick didn't know who he was. "The car fatality."

Bolick frowned. "You're from last night."

"That's me."

"Well look, my friend—"

"Frank Branco."

"—you did your good-citizenship bit. I thought I thanked you already, but maybe it slipped my mind. We got busy there. So, thanks a bunch, okay? Much obliged." Bolick stepped back from the door. "Now, if you don't mind . . ."

Frank did not move. Bolick gripped his belt and gave it a twist. "Guess you didn't catch me, my friend."

Quietly Frank said, "Let's cut the Barney Fife bullshit."

Bolick blinked. "What?"

"The guy in the crash last night was a former major-league ballplayer. Not that it matters. But I've been thinking about that crash all morning and most of the night. It doesn't add up."

"Now hold on here. What're you saying?"

"I walked up to the road there in daylight, where the car went through. There were no skid marks, nothing to say Frawley braked or swerved. Last night wasn't warm enough for AC or that cool either. So why were all his windows rolled up? And that fire . . . I've got questions about that."

Bolick drummed fingers on his belt and sized Frank up. Then he closed the office door. He waved Frank into a chair and took his own. "Where you from again?" he asked.

"Boston."

He didn't ask if Frank had played for the Red Sox. "What're you doing in Cooperstown?"

"Visiting the Corvette museum. Come on, why does anyone come to Cooperstown?"

Bolick's plump cheeks tightened.

"I won a trip. On the radio," Frank said. "I came up on Saturday."

"And you're a cop?"

"*Was.*"

Frowning, Bolick glanced toward the photos on his wall. Maybe they reminded him of who he still was. He took a different tack. "You have fun over the weekend, Mr. Branco?"

"Yes, I did."

"And at the game yesterday? It's a nice little town, isn't it? Peaceful?"

"A real slice of apple pie," Frank said, going along, meaning it.

"Aren't a lot of them left. All over the country"—Bolick made a broad gesture, indicating the world beyond his realm—"you got problems you didn't have fifteen, twenty years ago. Crime, drugs, violence you never used to see. Babies born with no fathers. It's been oozing out of the cities, invading practically everywhere. Not here though. This is one place that hasn't changed. Somebody dumps a sack of garbage on the road, or bolts a check at the Short Stop restaurant, that's a crime wave. This past weekend I had a bicycle patrol, and a couple of my six full-timers on plainclothes detail—making sure the vendors had the right licenses to sell hot dogs and souvenirs. Hey, maybe it'll come . . . maybe no place is immune forever, but I think about those boys who played baseball in the cow field back in 1839 . . . that started something that represents hope. You catch that series they had on the television? We get a half million visitors a year—people from all acrost America, around the world. White, black, young and old. And they come here in peace. I want it to stay that way."

Frank felt oddly moved by the man's words; they sounded earnest, and yet he wondered how many times Bolick had delivered them. "I'm with you," Frank said equably. "And if what happened last night was just an accident, then I'll say fine, I'm glad I'm wrong. But what if it wasn't? What if I'm not?"

Bolick pulled at his earlobe. "What do you mean?"

"When I leaned into that car last night, I smelled something I didn't identify. I've been thinking about it."

"What kind of smell?"

"Some kind of chemical, maybe—sweet with a kind of bite to it."

"And?"

"Suppose it was a fire starter."

Bolick frowned. "The acting fire marshal was there. If he suspected anything, he'd have said so."

"Have you examined the wreck in the daylight?"

"No, I just work here. Of *course* I have. The gas tank blew. What you probably smelled was gasoline."

"When will you get autopsy results?"

"What?"

"It's this thing they can do—examine a body and find out how the person died."

Bolick swore, jingled around the desk, and stood above Frank. "All right, smart guy—you were a cop once, maybe that's worth something. So I'll share this, just to take a little of that starch out of you." He settled on the edge of his desk. "Frawley wasn't even supposed to be driving. His license was lifted in Utica for third-offense DWI. Okay? That's for openers. Figure he drove down from there for old time's sake, got a little too loaded, and dozed off. He was drinking at a bar over in Fly Creek earlier last night. The stretch of road along the lake where he lost control is dark and tricky. People speed on it. The no skid marks makes sense if he passed out. We're damn lucky he didn't kill anyone but himself."

"I appreciate your sharing that," Frank said, trying to be persuasive. "So wouldn't an autopsy make sense? To confirm he was drunk?"

"The hell with that. Frawley's being buried tomorrow. His next of kin made the funeral arrangements himself, and he specifically said, *'No autopsy.'* Sweet Sonny Jesus, the guy was charcoal."

Frank swallowed, reminded of the distant glimpse he'd had of the driver after the fire. He and the chief were silent a moment, then Bolick sighed. "Look, you said you had some fun here. Go on back to Boston, Mr. Branco, okay? Take your memories and souvenirs. I asked my official questions and got my answers. This isn't a big city, I'll grant that; but we do a pretty fair job here. We keep the traffic flowing smoothly, keep parties from getting too rowdy, and we keep the peace. If there's a crime, we investigate, but we don't go around looking for something where it doesn't exist. There hasn't been a homicide here in twenty years. Still isn't. This matter is closed."

"Branco? Branc—oh, wow. Frank. Man, what can I say? Mea culpa in *spades*. I am like major-league chagrined."

Tom Webster sounded on the telephone just the way he did in person and, presumably, on the radio: hyped-up and about as genuine as you could expect. "I mean it. I am sorry about last night."

Frank knew he wasn't referring to the car crash and Herb Frawley's death, or having spilled his drink on Frank's coat. The sportscaster had passed out by the time of the wreck and was snoring by the lake's edge. Frank had driven him to the Otesaga Hotel. Webster was back in Utica now.

"When do you go on the air?" Frank asked.

Webster groaned. "Don't remind me. Drive time this afternoon—if I live that long."

"Have you got a news wire there?"

"Man, you should've shut me off. Did I do anything really dumb? News wire?"

"Or whatever you call it."

"At WENC? Come on, we're the Voice of the Mohawk Valley. What do you need?"

"Well—"

"Come on. You need something? I screwed up—I owe you."

It didn't sound like a guilt that would last much longer than the hangover; Frank knew he had better take advantage while he could.

3

THE BIRCH BARK LODGE, ON ROUTE 28 NOT FAR BEYOND the Cooperstown town line in Fly Creek, fits its name. A rustic wood-frame building with Adirondack chairs arrayed on the screened porch and Genesee beer signs in the windows, it had the look of a sportsmen's camp. Chief Bolick had refused to give the name of the bar, which was understandable—Frank couldn't argue against a public official not disclosing case data. What was irksome was the police chief's refusal to consider any other possibility than a drunk-driving mishap. Fortunately Fly Creek's options were limited, and Frank had got lucky at the one other bar he had tried. Last night's crash was as ready a topic of conversation as yesterday's game, and word had got out that the dead man had visited the Birch Bark Lodge sometime earlier in the evening.

At pine tables were a scattering of men who looked like they might be responsible for the trophy fish and trappers' gear affixed to the walls. Suspended from the bare joists over the bar hung a canoe, its birch bark hull yellowed with age. Behind the bar, a blond woman, pretty in a weathered way that fit the surroundings, let Frank get seated on a stool before she parked her cigarette in an ashtray and stepped over. They exchanged greetings and he ordered a Saranac Pale Ale. When she set the glass in front of him, he said, "How do you get away without any baseball memorabilia? Isn't there a law or something?" He had read in the official Hall of Fame yearbook that an old baseball found in a dusty attic in Fly Creek during the 1930s had buttressed the claim that the game had been played in these parts a century earlier.

"We're kind of out of step, huh?" the bartender said. "The truth is I hate baseball. Or I hate what it does to people," she added. "Turning wives into widows."

Frank took interest. "Widows?"

"April to October. And turns men to morons. The newspaper headline is screaming about Bosnia, or the government or a school bus wreck, and they crack the paper in half to read about the damn ball game they watched on TV last night." She shook her head, sighed. "Sorry, didn't mean to unload."

Frank grinned. "I'll bet you're not in the local booster club."

She snorted a laugh and went to tend to another customer. The ale was cold, and when the bartender brought Frank a second glass, he asked her, "Do you know who was tending bar last night?"

"Well, let's see—that'd either be me, or me."

"Can you pin it down any more than that?"

She smiled. "I own the place. Tess Hitchman."

"My name's Frank Branco. I'm a private investigator out of Boston."

The smiled vanished. Her eyes didn't leave his face as she stubbed her cigarette and whiffed the last smoke sideways. "Well, now, that didn't take long."

"For what?"

"Don't tell me. You're working for some lawyer to try to pin that man's death on me on account of he had a drink here, and someone smells money to be made. Well finish that beer and screw, because the thing I hate even more than baseball is goddamn lawyers."

"Whoa." Frank showed his palms. "I am here about Herb

Frawley, but no one hired me. And I'm not looking to blame any-one for anything."

Her faded blue eyes stayed skeptical. "What then?"

"I was at the accident scene. I tried to pull him out of the car before it burned."

Tess Hitchman gave a sympathetic frown. "That must've been rough. I read the paper. And you're not looking to make trouble?"

"I think the police chief in Cooperstown believes I am. He likes the drunk-driving idea because it's simple. Maybe he's right."

"What's your angle?"

"I just don't think anyone has looked long enough."

Tess Hitchman glanced around, then moved closer. "I'm not saying he wasn't drinking, but he had only one round here. Beer and an Irish Mist."

"How was he when he came in?"

"Not loaded. If anything he seemed stone sober."

"When was that?"

"Seven, maybe a little after."

Two hours before he crashed. "Do you know where he went when he left?"

"No."

"Did you notice anything else about him? His manner, maybe? Or something he said?"

The woman came nearer still, as if drawn by the challenge. "He seemed . . . expectant. Like he was waiting for somebody."

"Any idea who?"

"A woman, I would've said. Then he got a call—the phone back here." She gestured behind her. "It was a man asking for someone by name. The other patrons were regulars, so I asked if it was him. That's how I recognized the name when I saw it in the *Courier* this morning. I phoned up Cooperstown police so there'd be no questions."

"Do you know who telephoned Frawley?"

"Uh-uh. He just asked to speak to a patron and gave the name and described him. I put Mr. Frawley on, and a few minutes later he left. Didn't even finish all of his beer come to think of it."

"Did the police send someone out to talk to you this morning?"

"No. I spoke with Chief Bolick directly."

Tess Hitchman went over and took care of one of the tables of outdoorsmen and came back. She brought her cigarettes and got one going. Frank said, "Tess, had Frawley ever been in before?"

"You get so you can spot the first-timers. The way they walk in, kind of hesitant, look around. No, he'd never been in that I know of."

"Did you know he was a former baseball player?"

"I read that in the paper. It surprised me. He looked way out of shape."

When Frank had paid for the drinks and left a tip for the information, Tess Hitchman said, "Maybe it doesn't mean anything, but there's one other thing I just thought of. That poor guy seemed expectant, like I said, but he was also kind of . . ." Her hands sought a word. "Nervous."

"What do you mean?"

"Edgy, like he had something he had to do."

"Before or after the phone call?"

"Before. Afterward he didn't stick around." She squinted one eye. "Any of that helpful?"

"I don't know. The beer was tasty."

4

"THE POLICE CHIEF DIDN'T MENTION IT?" FRANK KEPT HIS
surprise out of the question.

"No, sir. You know how cop politics goes," Butch Huggins
said. "I don't imagine it's any different than Boston, except for the
scale of it."

They were riding in Huggins's shiny black Pathfinder through
the center of town, windows open to the cool morning air. Huggins
was the large young fireman who had been at the crash scene last
night—the *acting* fire chief, he'd explained, filling in while the regular chief had bypass surgery. He wore a handlebar mustache in the
same crisp orange hair that was on his head and on the big hands
that held the wheel in an easy grip. He reminded Frank of the
cutout cardboard figure that sat atop new cars in auto showrooms.

"I hope it's that," Frank said.

Huggins sent a glance Frank's way. "What do you mean?"

"Politics, and not sandbagging an investigation."

"The chief isn't a bad guy, just unimaginative. He thinks he's
lord of his own bucolic little realm. He's been around a lot longer
than I have. What did it smell like?"

"Chemical smell, with a bite to it. A solvent maybe. Bucolic?"

Huggins grinned. "I got me a set of those vocabulary tapes. Figure maybe I'll get to be president one day. Or permanent fire chief's okay too." He looked over again. "Not booze alcohol?"

That was one kind of solvent, Frank supposed. "I don't think so," he said.

Earlier Frank had driven out the narrow, tree-lined road that circled the lake and had found the place where Herb Frawley's Plymouth had gone through the woods last night. There was a sharp bend there, and ten yards off the shoulder, down a slope was a granite boulder which Frawley's car had narrowly missed. The car had cleared a path beside it, snapping off pine branches and tearing up ferns as it plowed through. Footprints said people had already been there, measuring and checking. In the sandy soil at the road's edge Frank had found a small dark stain of some kind and had sifted some of the soil in his hand and brought it to his nose. Expecting what? A chemical smell? What he'd got might have been the flat odor of engine oil.

Huggins drew into a Gulf station, making a bell ding inside the garage. He waved to someone in the office and kept going, driving around the side of the building to the rear. "Here we are," he declared, stopping. "Thar she blows."

Ahead, formed by an eight-foot chainlink fence topped with barbed wire, was an enclosure. It held a half dozen vehicles in various states of ruin. The lot backed onto a thick green tangle of woods. Huggins got out and unlatched the gate, and they walked in on crushed stone.

Some of the vehicles *looked* like death cars: crumpled by head-ons on farm roads like beer cans tossed aside by a bellicose drunk. The Plymouth had a different look. It stood along one side of the fenced enclosure, at the end of two deep furrows in the gravel where it had been towed in. In the daylight, except for the exploded rear portion and its scorched exterior, the car was remarkably intact. It was as if the windows, tires, and seats had been spirited away by midnight vandals who had spray-painted the body black. Replace those and give it a paint job, and you might almost drive it away. But that was illusion. The metal was so charred it gave the impression it might still be hot. It wasn't. Huggins leaned on the driver's door and looked inside. Cicadas chirred noisily from the tall trees crowding close to the back of the enclosure.

"What happens," Butch Huggins said, ducking back out of the car, "the fuel line ruptures, gasoline squirts on the hot block, forget it. The firewall holds the fire back from the passenger compartment awhile, so it sneaks along the underbody. Once flame reaches the fuel tank . . ." He banged on the roof to complete the idea. "Luckily there doesn't seem to have been much gas in the tank or more people might've been hurt."

The hood was crumpled just enough so that the catch was sprung and could not be opened. Frank squatted and peered through the gap-toothed grille. There were splinters of charred wood caught in there, and something else caught his eye. He took his pen and poked it through and knocked out a fragment of brown glass. He examined it, then glanced up at Huggins. "Got a crowbar?"

Huggins fetched a tire iron from the Pathfinder and popped the hood. In the collapsed space between the grille and the engine, they found two more shards of melted brown glass.

"Could've been just a misplaced beer bottle, maybe from the gazebo," Huggins said, as if a counter to what Frank found himself thinking: a bottle containing something flammable set in the space, which on impact could splash over the manifold.

Frank rubbed a mosquito from his hand. "Odd place for it. Could you have it tested?"

"Somebody said they thought they saw you, Branco."

Chief Bolick's belt hadn't announced him this time. He came through the gate, his fleshy face shadowed by the brim of his campaign hat. Huggins stepped away from the burned Plymouth. "Morning, Chief."

"Butch," Bolick greeted, but was looking at Frank. "What's going on?"

"Well, Mr. Branco thought he smelled something last night, Chief," Huggins said.

"I smelled something too. Like you'd been saucing, Branco. We've been there already. I'll get back to you on this, Butch. I'll give Mr. Branco a lift to his hotel."

Huggins shrugged and went out and got into the Pathfinder and drove off. Wordlessly, Bolick watched him go. The bell rang faintly inside the garage again.

"It isn't his fault," Frank said. "I talked him into coming."

Bolick turned and moved a few steps sideways. Frank was forced to squint into the sun through the trees. It occurred to him that these were the same woods that James Fenimore Cooper had long ago inhabited with mystery and danger, and whose family had given the town its name.

"Yeah, well, he's just temporary as chief," Bolick said. "And this place is off-limits to you. I figured an ex-cop would know that."

"Why? I thought the car wasn't criminal evidence."

"It isn't. It's private property."

"There's no harm done."

"Let's go. I'll take you back to your hotel, so you can pack."

"Running me out of town, Chief? That's a little melodramatic, isn't it?"

Bolick hooked his thumbs into his belt, and leveled his eyes with Frank's. "You think I'm screwing with you, Branco?"

"I don't know. Are you?"

Now a faint, almost lazy movement lifted a corner of the chief's mouth. Was it an ironic smile? "When you told me you'd been a cop back there in Boston, you didn't mention anything about you getting shot," Bolick said. "Or about Maximo Diaz."

Until now Frank's feeling about the police chief had mostly been impatience, and a certain doubt about his competence; but all at once he felt a sharp hatred toward the man and, grudgingly, a new respect. "You never asked," Frank said.

5

JAMES BOLICK HAD DRIVEN HIM BACK TO THE INN, TELLING
Frank that with just six full-time officers and a small part-time staff,
the village of Cooperstown police weren't in a position to conduct
a murder investigation, even if they believed it was warranted,
which they didn't. That would fall to the New York State Police
and the Otsego County Sheriff's Department. If Frank wanted to
take responsibility for going to them, on the basis of unsupported
hunches, Bolick pointed out, he was free to do so, though he would
not get Bolick's support. Frank had declined the offer.

The ride north to Utica took just under an hour, during which
Frank had mulled the notion of just getting on the thruway to
Boston, but he hadn't done that either.

Tom Webster was bleary-eyed and unshaven, dressed in jeans
and a faded black T-shirt that said Lollapalooza '92 Tour, Saratoga
Springs. He was gulping coffee from a mug, priming himself to
go on air. "Christ, I didn't miss any fireworks last night," he said.
"I got them all right here in my skull. Why didn't you shut me
off?"

He and Frank were seated across from each other at a battered

Formica-top table in a tiny production room at WENC, Voice of the Mohawk Valley.

A cute brunette strolled by and smiled with a twenty-year-old's version of lasciviousness. "Hi, Tommy."

Webster swallowed more coffee. "Get my intro cued up, will you, sweetheart?"

The girl went into the broadcast booth. Frank watched her through the soundproof glass going through a rack of what looked like eight-track tapes. "Intern from SUNY," Webster said. "She totally wants my bod."

Frank turned back to him. "Herb Frawley," Frank said.

Webster scrubbed a hand over his tired, sunburned face. "Yeah, okay. I checked the news files for you. Frawley lived in town the last ten years or so. Nothing really newsworthy till last night."

Frank scanned a page of notes and stats Webster had jotted: an only slightly expanded version of what the baseball book and the obituary had told him. He did learn that Frawley's son, Jason, was thirty and lived in New York City. There was no mention of Frawley's brother. Webster said, "I also talked to a friend who works at a bank here. She gave me this on the Q.T. Frawley had a passbook savings account there which shows little activity, regular monthly deposit of a few hundred. Then, seven months ago, in January, one blast. He put in close to twelve thousand bucks. Cash."

Frank sat forward. "Any explanation for it?"

"No. His biggest expense, from what I gather, must've been booze. He had three DWIs and lost his license for good last November. Like that means a lot, huh?"

"What do you mean?"

"It didn't keep him away from driving down and crashing our party last night. I wish it'd been sooner, for my sake. Come on, did I do anything *really* dumb?"

"I don't think anyone remembers much before the car crash."

Webster shook his head and drank more coffee.

"Anything else on Herb Frawley?" Frank asked.

"What's the big interest? You know the guy?"

"No."

"Well, he had a hell of a year for the Giants in fifty-six."

He had. According to the statistics Webster had listed, in his first full season in the majors, Frawley hit nineteen home runs, had seventy-eight RBIs, batted .315, and stole twenty-one bases. And the next year he had started even hotter, but he played only ninety-one games for New York before being traded to Detroit in late July. But stats were just numbers on paper; they didn't reveal much. Frank thanked Tom Webster, folded the page of notes, put it in his pocket, and rose.

Beyond the window in the air studio, the college intern who was hot for Webster's bod pointed at Webster and pushed a thick cassette into a machine. The clock on the wall behind her showed 4 P.M. There was a heavy guitar intro, which quickly faded down behind sounds of cheering, as if a vast and supercharged crowd had assembled. Webster held out his hand. "Adios, amigo. Gotta go."

"Win one for the Gipper," Frank said. As he left he heard the canned cheering subside and Webster's voice rise on the studio monitors, a bright, high-octane sound that didn't match the hung-over appearance: "Hey there, sports animals!"

The rooming house was on the south side of the city, a tired Victorian with elm trees shadowing the patchy front yard and a paved area at one end designated as tenant parking. Frank left the Taurus on the street. The prize package for the Fan's Fantasy Weekend had included a subcompact rental, which he had upgraded to give his bad leg extra room, though as he got out now, the leg was as limber as a flagpole.

On the wraparound porch there were chairs set out, and potted geraniums, and red cans for butts, but no one was enjoying the amenities. The dry heat of early August held sway. Frank rapped on the thick oval plate of glass in the front door. Behind him, late-afternoon traffic swished by on Genesee Street. He had gotten the address from Tom Webster and had called information for the telephone number. He had phoned from the radio station. Webster had given him directions.

A face peered out from behind age-browned curtains, then the door opened. A woman who looked to be in her mid-seventies stood there, brushing gray hair back from a flushed brow. She was dressed in black, but Frank doubted it was for the occasion. "Mrs. Talarico?"

"The man on the phone? Come in. Terrible about Mr. Frawley. He was a nice man."

Frank followed her down a linoleum hallway into a kitchen where an enamel stove was giving off blast-furnace heat, fragrant with garlic. "I'm getting dinner ready for my boarders," the woman said.

Frank hoped they appreciated it; he was already sweating.

Mrs. Talarico checked something in the oven, then got a key off a hook. "Mr. Frawley wasn't in trouble with the police, was he?"

"No, ma'am. I happened to be there when he crashed," he told her again. "I've spoken with the Cooperstown police. They know I'm a trained investigator."

Meaning what? she might well have asked. She didn't. Talking all the way, she led him up a stairway and along a hallway to a door with a number 8 on it. There was a six-pack carton of Utica Club outside the door, five empty bottles in it. "He walked out each day to return the bottles and would get some more," she explained as she unlocked the door.

"Every day?"

"Always said hello when he saw me. Never no problem at all. A nice man."

"Had he lived here long?"

"Ten years." She opened the door and stepped back, and Frank understood that this was as far as she was going. "You gonna take his stuff?" she asked.

"No," Frank said.

She nodded cheerlessly. "His brother didn't either."

"Mr. Frawley's brother was here?"

"This morning. A quiet gentleman, older than him. Just looked around awhile and left." Mrs. Talarico glanced past Frank into the room and crossed herself. "Stay as long as you like," she said. "I'll be down in my kitchen if you need me."

Herb Frawley's home was a tired, wallpapered room full of trapped heat, even with the single window open—the kind of room that would be icy with drafts in winter. Take away the faded carpet, the curtains on the window, and the furniture, which Mrs. Talarico had said came with the rent, and there wasn't much: a tiny refrigerator, a TV with foil bow ties on its rabbit ears, a VCR, some magazines, a small unframed print of Edward Hopper's *Nighthawks*. So Frank had expected what? Old pennants from the Polo Grounds? Crisscrossed Louisville Sluggers? Remembering Tess Hitchman's comment about Frawley not looking like a ballplayer when he had visited the Birch Bark Lodge last night, Frank experienced a small lethargy of disappointment. Overcoming it, he began to search the room.

He worked systematically, in the way he had learned as a Boston cop, and again with the department's underwater recovery unit, where the dark murk of the harbor made thoroughness essential. He began on the wall with the window. He checked each drawer in the dresser, sifting through the scant personal belongings Frawley had owned. A small toilet bag contained razor, toothbrush, and other items. Meaning he hadn't intended on staying overnight in Cooperstown? He looked behind the dresser for anything that might have fallen down. Nothing had.

The short stack of mail on the bed table told little, as did the assortment of clothes and shoes in Frawley's closet. A plastic wastebasket held only a few used strands of dental floss. In the tabletop refrigerator a wedge of blue cheese announced its presence. Frank developed an image of a person who could be extravagant in the way only a poor man can: on impulse investing in an imported silk pocket square to go with a cheap sport coat, lizard-skin boots, a filet mignon that he consigned to the freezer.

Among some outdated magazines on the shelf of the TV stand was an unopened mailer bag, addressed to Frawley. Debating for a moment, Frank pulled the little paper tab and zipped open the package. Inside was a videocassette, with a brief thank-you-for-your-purchase form letter and a small catalog of films. The package was from a place called Black Satin Underground in New York City. Frank put the tape into the deck. Funky music came on, then two naked men and two naked women doing things to themselves and each other. He watched, feeling in an odd way his first real link with the man whom he had tried to pull from the burning car. Frank let the tape run for another minute, then ejected it. The title of the work was *Lady with a Feather*.

Twenty minutes of searching brought Frank back to where he had begun, and not much closer to an understanding of Herb Frawley. That nettled him, ran counter to his belief that the places where people lived (and loved and sometimes hurt each other) bore witness to them, were haunted by their subtlest ghosts. What had eluded him here? He sat on the bed, letting his mind fray out for a few moments; but nothing came. He felt as ineffectual as the lonely figures in the Hopper painting.

As he was leaving, he glanced down at the five empty bottles in the carton in the hall, and now an idea did prod him.

He opened the tiny refrigerator again. No sixth bottle of beer. Hypothetical question: Had the bottle ended up in the engine compartment of Frawley's car? The idea stirred him for a moment, but then it came apart. Who would have put the bottle there? Going out, Frank looked at the five empties. One day's worth. Maybe Bolick was right.

The kitchen's aromas had intensified, making Frank's mouth water. Mrs. Talarico was setting a long table. Frank mentioned the food still in Herb Frawley's refrigerator; she said she was going to clean the room after the funeral and would probably send Frawley's things to his son.

"Did Mr. Frawley keep up with his rent?" Frank inquired.

"Always. He gave me a check on the first of the month. He's paid up through the first of September."

Frank didn't correct her use of the present tense. "Did he have much money?"

"I wouldn't know that. Like I say, he paid up regular."

"Had he been in any kind of trouble lately that you could tell?"

"Trouble?" She set down a fork and looked at him like the question had no meaning.

"Or depressed?"

"He always had a friendly hello whenever he seen me."

"How about visitors?"

"His son a few times—a quiet young man, but not lately. Today his brother I told you about. Practically none of my borders have visitors, and if they do they have to park on the street."

Frank glanced through one of the large windows at the paved side lot. "Do your boarders have assigned spaces?"

The woman pointed out Frawley's spot, beneath an elm tree. "But he didn't drive much," she said.

"No?"

"That's why I was surprised when he left last night, driving out of here fast like he done." She opened the oven with a pot holder and squinted in, the heat making her gray hair shimmer. "You like stuffed manicotti? Mr. Frawley did. Said my food was the best he'd ever eaten, and he'd traveled all over. Even lived down Mexico awhile. He used to be a baseball player."

In the parking area beside the rooming house, Frank stood in the space where Herb Frawley's Plymouth used to sit. There was a greasy patch on the pavement, the result, over time, of a persistent engine leak. He thought about the stain in the sand near where the car had crashed through the woods in Cooperstown. Was it possible both stains were from the same source? Meaning what? That Frawley's car had been parked there on the shoulder for a time, before the crash?

As he started back to his own car, Frank glanced up at the window to Herb Frawley's room, and something caught his eye.

Mrs. Talarico let him take the key up and let himself in this time. Frank went to the window and found what had drawn his attention from the parking lot. Propping the sash open, half-hidden from inside by the curtain, was a brown Utica Club bottle. Number six? A slant of afternoon light revealed something inside it. Removing the bottle, he lowered the sash on the assortment of mummified insects on the sill. He shook a piece of rolled paper out of the bottle.

It was a typewritten note, three lines:

> What's a career worth?
> A grand a year?
> Send thirty-five in cash.

Frank stared at it, drawn into a maze of thought he hadn't entered before. Around him the air seemed to drone at last with the ghosts of the drab room. Had Herb Frawley's trap been something more than a burning car? Was the career reference to Frawley's time in the majors, thirty-five years ago? Was this why the man had lived so meanly? Because his money was going somewhere else? With a rising excitement, Frank smoothed the note and put it in his pocket. He set the bottle into the carton with the other five as he left.

6

HERB FRAWLEY HAD NOT HAD A LOT OF FRIENDS. NOT, AT least, if you measured friendship in terms of who showed up for your burial. Counting the funeral home's two royal blue Fleetwoods, the cortege was seven cars long. For Maximo Diaz's funeral in Mattapan, the Boston police had needed special details to handle the traffic.

Frank watched the cars come up the slope and move crisply among the lanes of grass and stone of Forest Lawn Cemetery. He had learned the location from yesterday's Utica newspaper. He had stayed overnight at a motel out on the interstate, lulled to sleep finally by the whine of highway traffic. He had come early and now kept a discreet distance, pretending to read old gravestones as he watched the burial party. He counted a dozen guests, one of whom was Mrs. Talarico, the landlady, whose widow's weeds fit the occasion. There were a few handkerchiefs, though they seemed meant more to catch the odd sneeze brought on by the drift of summer pollen than by any visible outpouring of grief. It was early, and the trees cut some of the heat, but like the cortege the ceremony had gone a little faster than these things tended to, as if this were something everyone wanted done with. Afterward, the pastor and all but two of the mourners retreated to the cars, which promptly began taking them away in air-conditioned silence.

One of the two people remaining, a man who looked to be in his early thirties, bent to drop a red rose into the open grave. The other person, a woman in a gray dress, who might have been the same age, approached the man. Her hair showed golden under a small gray hat. She spoke to the man, causing him to straighten and, without a glance, stride off. He headed toward the remaining cars, moving purposefully. When the woman didn't follow, Frank moved to intersect his path.

He was tall and slender, with neat brown hair and a sparse mustache. "Would you be Herb Frawley's son?" Frank asked.

The man stopped. He was perspiring, and his dark blue eyes measured Frank warily. "Who are you?"

Frank introduced himself. The young man's lips moved, silently replaying the name. "You're the one on the accident report. The police chief told me about you. You tried to pull him out."

Though Frank doubted it would have made much difference, he said, "I wish I could've managed it."

The young man glanced away. He seemed to be trying to chew the corners of his mustache, but there wasn't enough of it. Frank said, "You are his son?"

"Jason Frawley, yes. But what I—" Jason Frawley's attention had been taken by something behind Frank. Without another word, he spun and abruptly marched away. Turning, Frank saw the woman in the gray dress approaching.

"Jason," she called, but Jason was hurrying down an aisle between gravestones, toward the cars. Only a small station wagon and one of the blue Cadillacs remained.

"Were you here for the funeral?"

The woman was addressing Frank. He turned to her. "Well . . . technically, yes."

The woman was older than she had looked at a distance. Early fifties, Frank guessed now. She was pretty, with dark blue eyes, her suntanned face darkened by her golden hair and white teeth. Her expression might have been puzzlement, or distaste.

"I never knew Herb," Frank said. "I happened to be there the other night when he died."

"You were *with* him?"

"At the party where the crash occurred." Then he added, "I'm an investigator."

"You're investigating the accident?"

"Not officially, no."

She looked after the young man, then at Frank. "Did Jason say anything?"

"Not much. He seemed in a hurry."

"Did he hire you?"

"No one has," Frank admitted. "I take it you know Jason Frawley."

The woman glanced down, fingering the rough-cut crest of a gravestone. When she looked at Frank, her eyes were dark and intense. He felt their scrutiny, or perhaps it was accusal; he hadn't intended to invade anyone's grief. She said, "Mr.—"

"Branco," he told her.

"Is there anything wrong concerning Herb's death?"

"I don't know. I have some questions."

"Was he drunk?"

"I'm told he was. I don't know. Were you a friend of his?"

She looked toward the two cars again and raised a gloved hand. An older man who was waiting beside the Cadillac came to life. He got in behind the wheel.

"Questions about what?" the woman asked.

"His being drunk, for one," Frank said. "There's a bartender who says he wasn't when he left her bar. The crash, for another thing."

"What do you mean?"

"It's possible it wasn't an accident."

"Really?"

High in a tree a cicada complained of the heat. The woman's gray dress was expensive—silk, which would breathe and keep its wearer cool, unlike his polyester blazer. Frank resisted an urge to wipe his brow. Sunlight made patterns on the grass, and on the deep blue sheen of the Cadillac as it drew alongside Frank and the woman. As the driver came around, the woman snapped open her small purse and took out a card, which she looked at, then handed to Frank. The driver held open the rear passenger-side door. "I'd like to talk about this," the woman said. "I have to go—I've got a flight to make. Would you call me in a couple of days?"

Only after the driver had closed the door and the car had rolled quietly away did Frank look at the card. It was for an art gallery in Provincetown on Cape Cod, and the woman was Nola Dymmoch, a name Frank knew from the obituary. She had once been Mrs. Herb Frawley.

7

"It was the last game of spring training in fifty-seven. Frawley went four for four against the Phils, and the Giants won five-two in Sarasota."

Frank shook his head in wonder. "You did well."

Ty Gilchrist's thick shoulders moved. "It doesn't take Sherlock Holmes. Baseball is a numbers game. People who can't play, count. And they keep track." He handed the old scorecard to Frank. "That's worth ten bucks as ephemera."

"Ephemera?" The word made Frank think of butterflies.

"That's what the dealer said on the phone. Said you should seal it in plastic too."

Gilchrist sat in profile against the fading sky beyond the window. Somewhere a police siren wailed faintly, a familiar enough sound for Boston's South End, though not one Frank had ever gotten used to at a distance. Sitting in a car that was making the sound gave a sense that you had some control; however, that was largely an illusion, Frank had discovered. In a corner of the room a television was on: the Red Sox and the Rangers.

"Sentiment," Frank said.

Gilchrist turned his head slightly, which meant his torso moved too. "For cop cars and night patrols?"

"For *Frawley's* salad days, not mine." Frank lurched out of his chair, restless, though in the small apartment there wasn't much room to move in. "Is that why he kept the scorecard in his wallet? An old reminder?"

"He was on a streak then. He had a hot bat. But it didn't last. That was April, he got traded in July and wound up the season hitting one-seventy-three for De-troit."

"*De*-troit?"

"Yeah, like *be*-ah." Gilchrist held up his empty bottle. Frank fetched a replacement.

If you didn't look below the waist, you could well believe that Tyrone Gilchrist had been a two-time All-Pro wide receiver for the Pats. Frank retained video images of him as a downfield flash, swift as a cat at something like six-three, 225 pounds, with hands a pickpocket would envy. From deep in Delta Mississippi originally, he had made Boston his home ever since his unplanned retirement from the NFL. Frank had met him in the flesh at a rehabilitation class at Boston City Hospital. His head seemed carved out of dark stone, as fierce and mystical as a monolith on a remote Pacific island. Drop your eyes, though, to what stayed between the stainless steel rails of the electric wheelchair, and you knew something had gone terribly awry. Gilchrist's two halves did not seem to belong together. Factor in the mind occupying his head, and that was a whole other thing.

Leaning toward the TV screen for light, Frank looked again at the stat sheet Gilchrist had assembled from one of the dozens of sports books that filled shelves in his apartment: football, basketball, golf, boxing, baseball.

YEAR	TEAM	GAMES	AB	H	HR	RBI	AVG.	SB
1955	NYGiants	9	22	9	1	3	.409	2
1956	NYGiants	141	489	154	19	78	.315	21
1957	NYGiants	91	353	114	13	52	.323	17
1957	Detroit	45	162	28	3	8	.173	2
1958	Detroit	144	518	122	9	43	.235	7
1959	Detroit	72	195	38	4	13	.195	3
1960	Chi(N)	101	242	58	6	33	.240	8
1961	Chi(N)	35	60	13	2	7	.217	2
1961	L.A.	46	147	33	2	15	.224	2
Major League Totals		684	2,188	569	59	252	.258	64

Frank set the sheet aside. Earlier he had come bearing gifts: a souvenir Colorado Rockies cap from Cooperstown, which Gilchrist now wore, and a six-pack of Belgian beer—along with the score-card from Herb Frawley's wallet, and the note he had found in a beer bottle in Frawley's rented room. Two were gifts anyway; the other two were work. Gilchrist liked to keep occupied. Frank always offered to pay him a researcher's fee, and Gilchrist always laughed. The NFL Players Association pension saw to his wants far better than any Boston PI ever could, thank you very much. As for living here—where the neighborhood bird was the jailbird, Gilchrist liked to say, and rats had totemic status—it was either this or one of the slick suburbs where most pro athletes set up house-keeping, and Gilchrist had been there. Ask him. Here he headed a city wheelchair basketball team, was adviser to this, patron of that. Wheelchairman of the board, he called himself.

"What about the note?" Frank asked.

Gilchrist's slabbed shoulders moved again. "Four teams in six seasons, then Frawley was out. Doesn't put much weight behind your blackmail idea. Who shakes down a two-fifty-eight lifetime hitter with no bank account and a thirst for Utica Club?"

And it occurred then to Frank that that was why he needed Gilchrist: a backboard for the angle shots of his own mind. He had driven two hundred miles home from Cooperstown without grasping the possibility that Frawley hadn't received the note, but rather had *written* it.

"Could be," Gilchrist said when Frank voiced it now.

"He went down to Cooperstown on a suspended license. The bartender at the Birch Bark Lodge said Frawley seemed expectant, and then he got a phone call and left. A couple hours later he was ashes. Maybe he was in Cooperstown for the payoff—and somebody stopped him."

Gilchrist grunted.

"It's possible," Frank insisted.

"So who was he shaking down?"

"The note says a thirty-five-year career. A Hall of Fame player, maybe."

"That cuts it down some. Only about sixty players in the Hall still among the living. You're still looking at a lot of names."

Frank felt his inspiration swimming away. Hot summer nights in the city could do that. Gilchrist turned to the television screen. He had the sound off, preferring to do commentary in his head. From time to time he took the beer bottle from between his withered thighs and drank. Frank was thinking about the twelve thousand dollars that had turned up suddenly in Frawley's bank account last winter, when Gilchrist said: "Four."

"What?"

"Two Willies, an Al, and a Jack."

"Translate."

"Nobody *plays* thirty-five years, so we look at someone going back that far. Mays, McCovey, Kaline, and Livingstone. Those are the four guys Frawley both played with and who are in the Hall."

It was the kind of statistical parlor trick Gilchrist could perform all night.

"Okay, good." Frank was enthusiastic again. "So what next? I can't call up any of them and ask him if he was being blackmailed. There has to be another angle."

Maybe thinking to find it, Gilchrist motored closer to the window and peered out. Night had fully come now. An east wind stirred the curtains and brought the smell of the sea. "You're going on hunches," he said. "Cop hunches, yeah, but they're still worth zero unless you've got something to sell. No one else seems to be losing sleep."

"So why should *I*?"

"You miss the game."

"The game?"

"The street game."

"Sometimes."

"Get me a beer."

Frank went into the apartment's kitchenette and got two more bottles of the Stella Artois, green and pebbled with fine moisture, and pried the tops off. On Gilchrist's list of requirements were that a beer could not come in a can nor could its cap be twisted off. Beer tasted best poured in a glass so it could breathe, but he broke too many glasses so he had quit using them. Beer was beer from Frank's standpoint; he hadn't met many he didn't like.

Gilchrist had played six seasons until a blind-side hit had put him in the wheelchair forever. The player who had hit him had boasted of the fact in a self-serving autobiography (was there any other kind?), but if there was bitterness in Ty Gilchrist, Frank had never detected it. Gilchrist took the cold bottle and set it between his thighs, an action which always made Frank wince; but you could have driven nails in those legs and not gotten a reaction.

"Wouldn't be a big deal finding out if any of those four was in Cooperstown for the induction last weekend," Gilchrist said. "A phone call would do it. But it still won't prove anything."

It wouldn't, Frank agreed. And yes, it was well possible Herb Frawley could have gotten snookered between leaving the Birch Bark and crashing the party two hours later. Frank watched the silent ball game. He felt the weariness of the long drive home from Utica, the tranquilizing effect of the beers. For some reason he found himself replaying his high school night game, an event he had not thought about in years, but which the Hall of Fame visit had reawakened. After all this time there was still a low heat of old regret at his failure . . . only now the kid in the outfield drifting in to catch the ball was not Frank but Maximo Diaz. There was a gunshot and someone toppled into a puddle, then Frank was there, holding a face underwater . . . or, no, pulling it *up*. Frank came awake as the beer started to spill.

Gilchrist sat in the TV glow across the dark room, a Buddha in canvas and stainless steel. Had the gunshot sound been the crack of a bat? Somewhere across the city, a siren keened. "Who's winning?" Frank mumbled.

"Game ended an hour ago. Rangers. This is a *Hill Street* rerun."

Frank set the bottle on the floor. "Who's winning?"

"Too early to say yet. Go home get some sleep, man. You're supposed to be on vakay."

8

SO FOR TWO DAYS FRANK TRIED TO BEHAVE LIKE A MAN
with the luxury of time to spend. He read; he stocked his larder;
he arranged his record and tape collection—getting organized, as
his ex-roommate of six years had frequently urged him to do. He
didn't think about Herb Frawley. He did think some about his ex-
roommate.

Kate was the one who had maintained that a marriage license
was just one more civic intrusion and had nothing to do with what
they felt for each other, though clearly its absence had made things
easier in the end when she decamped, taking with her, Frank discovered now, some of his favorite old blues albums (though she *had*
left her Donna Summer records, so probably she had seen it as a
fair exchange). It was also Kate who had put him onto Gilchrist,
which maybe, just maybe, had saved him. But being saved demanded first being lost, and Frank had managed that by himself.

The incident had begun with a radio dispatch on a rainy night,
nearly three years ago: a man prowling in an alley behind dwellings
on Marlborough Street. Frank, with his rookie partner, had responded. Stationing the partner to watch the front of the buildings,

Frank went into the dark alley. He let his vision adjust, moving carefully. Suddenly trash cans were being kicked over; there was a curse, a gunshot. Something tore through his leg, just below the knee. As Frank fell, a man came running toward him carrying a TV. Frank managed to grab a foot, but the guy was wiry, adrenalized, and they had struggled, smashing the TV, knocking over more trash cans, splashing in a big puddle. Frank finally got the man down, holding him. . . .

Maximo Diaz, it came out later, was seventeen, with an IQ of dull normal and a wizardry with electronics. An "idiot savant" the *Herald*, with its trademark unconcern for political correctness, called him. He had also been unarmed. The gunshot had been fired by Frank's rookie partner, who had followed procedures up to a point and then, apparently, had panicked, turning Frank's knee to spaghetti. The TV set Maximo Diaz had been carrying proved to be a castoff left in the alley with the trash. The death was determined to be accidental drowning: Diaz, an asthmatic, had aspirated water as he and Frank had struggled in the puddle. Frank's effort to resuscitate him had failed.

So you played what-if games, wondering what if you had taken a comp day that day since you had a deep pile accrued that were going to be lost if you didn't use them, or why you hadn't gone around the other way and therefore missed the puddle, or why it had rained in the first damn place, or what idiot put a TV out for trash, or why had the kid been so fucking dumb as to be alley-combing at midnight, and what if your partner had just obeyed you, and on and on, spinning out endless combinations of lost possibility; but any way you played it, Maximo Diaz was dead and nothing changed that. The rookie partner was discharged (working security at a junior college in Vermont at last report). Frank, with a nine-year record of good service, was cleared of any wrongdoing. But six months after the incident, he still could not walk without a cane nor sleep through the night nor feel any true desire for Kate—and there was no faking it with Kate. He tried a desk assignment, then volunteered for the underwater recovery unit, perhaps drawn more by the name than by the work of probing the murk of Boston Harbor for handguns and corpses. Finally, a year after the incident, he left the force. He did not return calls from the *Herald* and the *Globe*, but he could have told them what you did in such cases as his. You got up each day. You listened to blues records and you moped about and you drank; and each month you sent a note to the family of the dead youth, not out of any hope of forgiveness, or even a reply, but as a gesture of sorrow, and finally your best friend had had enough and left. But not before she gave you a phone number.

Frank had called the number and gone to the rehab class at Boston City Hospital. At first it was with an idea of getting Kate back, but that didn't happen, and he found himself just going. This big black guy would wheel in and speak to the group, his riff being that you could stay in the Mutual Aid Society of Losers long as you wanted, but there was life after a crippling injury. One time he showed a film clip of the blind-side hit that had sat him in his chair permanently. Frank was far from the worst off of the group—most had some kind of paralysis or had had amputations—but trauma can go deep beyond muscle and bone, and that was where Gilchrist's understanding was at its keenest. He played the film clip in slow motion, and speeded up, backward, and with a funky R & B track, so it became absurd, a Charlie Chaplin routine, and Gilchrist had laughed first, and last, and definitely the hardest. So putting Frank in touch, indirectly, with Ty Gilchrist had been an act of grace on Kate's part (and maybe hauling off the sad songs had been well-intentioned too, though the blues was one of the things which would later forge friendship between the two men). The lesson was that there were times when you had to take a hand.

On the third day of vacation, the seventh of August, Frank dug out the card that Herb Frawley's ex-wife had handed him at Forest Lawn Cemetery in Utica. He made a phone call. Then he packed a toothbrush and some clothes into his purple Patagonia bag and drove to Cape Cod.

PART TWO

ROAD TRIP

9

PROVINCETOWN WAS IN FULL SUMMER SWING: CROWDED, sun-drenched, and spiced with the smells of the sea. Part fishing village, part artist colony, P-town was situated at the tip of the land, and thus was a receptacle for flotsam and jetsam. Drag queens, bikers, beachcombers, fishermen, and tourists collected here and mingled in a rich bouillabaisse. Frank parked in a municipal lot by the tall Pilgrim Monument tower and walked into the busy streets. He got directions from a shirtless man with a gold hoop hung from one nipple. The Dymmoch Gallery was a surprisingly sedate old building of gray clapboard, with big windows facing Commercial Street. A sign in one of them announced, COMING: NEW WORK BY STEN NORDGREN and gave a date a week away.

After the sunlight of the street outside, Frank needed a moment for his eyes to adjust. When they had, they took in the polished hardwood floors, high ceilings, and plain white walls, adorning which were paintings: dozens of them, big squares of pale canvas on which someone apparently had dribbled paint and outlined the dribbles with ink. He went past a side gallery, where a stepladder stood near a wall where paintings were being hung.

He stopped. The images hung there were of men and women, in pairs and small groups, some bound and gagged, others dancing in wild abandon. All of the figures were nude. Getting over his initial surprise, Frank went into the room and approached one of the paintings. It depicted two men and a woman, arranged in such a way as to seem to be stalking each other. The anatomical details were precise, photographic almost—except for the faces. The faces were blurred, made slightly nightmarish, as if something had frightened the painter, causing his brush to jerk at the moment he painted them.

"Magnetic, isn't it?"

Frank turned to find a young woman at his shoulder. She had ink black hair brushed with a streak of purple, pale skin, and dark solemn eyes engaging his in a direct stare. "Are you a fan of Nordgren?" she asked.

He felt himself flush, though whether at his lack of knowledge or at sharing the content of the painting with the young woman, he wasn't sure. She might have been twenty, though her black garb and chalky complexion gave her an ageless appearance. He cleared his throat. "I don't know his work."

"You need to," she said intently. "He's just had shows in Key West and Tokyo, and he'll be opening here in a few days." The young woman drew closer, her voice alive with quiet urgency. "His dominant theme is power—its containment and release. The human form is a vessel for the most potent energies. Ambition, lust, violence. We contain them with social convention. The images suggest a world that exists at the very edges. Blake says the Palace of Wisdom is reached by the road of excess. Nordgren explores that road." She stopped abruptly and handed Frank a brochure.

It was an announcement for the exhibit scheduled to open in a week, a glossy double-fold affair. "I gather you work here," he said.

"Summers. I'm Zoe."

"Hi. Frank Branco. I'm supposed to meet Mrs. Dymmoch. Is she around?"

Zoe pulled herself from the paintings and directed him to a glassed office area at the rear of the gallery. He went back to it, trying to keep his glance away from the canvases on the walls, but not fully successfully. In that, Zoe was right: they did possess a power.

Inside the office, with her back to him, stood a blond woman, talking on a telephone. She had on a pale blue leotard and a denim skirt. Please, not another college student, he thought. Hearing his approach, the woman turned. She saw him and waved him in. It took him a moment to realize she was the woman he had met briefly at Herb Frawley's funeral in Utica: Frawley's ex-wife, Nola Dymmoch. Away from the solemnity of the graveyard, she looked years younger, though definitely not college age. There were tiny crow's-feet around her dark blue eyes, and the hint of smile lines at her mouth.

After another few seconds of waiting, she left a message on someone's answering machine, begging off from some social event being held at Norman's. Mailer? Frank wondered; the Boston papers often linked the writer with P-town. She hung up and held out her hand, smiling. "Mr. Branco. Thank you for coming. I'm glad you called." She was as bright and open as her young employee was dark and solemn. She looked at the brochure in his hand. "I see Zoe got you."

"She's pretty intense."

"Zoe's like a daughter I never had. This is her second summer at the gallery. She's an art history major at Vassar."

"Maybe I should've worn my beret."

Mrs. Dymmoch laughed. "Let me just return one other call, then I'm yours. Are you up for a stroll on the beach?"

A rear exit from the gallery led them down a flight of stairs to a small sunny crescent of beach. Tiny waves lapped on coarse yellow sand where seagulls and terns found lunch. Mrs. Dymmoch had donned sunglasses and a straw hat with a wide brim. Her sandals flapped softly, spilling sand. Frank tried to manage in Hush Puppies.

"What do you think of the work?" Mrs. Dymmoch asked.

"The work?"

"In the gallery."

"Well, I wouldn't go by my judgment."

"I've got to consider it. I'm not in business to fail."

"To tell the truth, I didn't see much of it. Only the paintings your assistant was hanging."

"Ah, Sten Nordgren. What do you think of him?" She was watching him with amusement and curiosity.

"I don't know about all that action, containment stuff. Those are paintings, huh? Taken from photos?"

"Nordgren works from life."

Frank tried to imagine models in the poses he had seen. The idea dazzled him a little. "I'll have to read this," he said, and folded the brochure into his shirt pocket.

Mrs. Dymmoch said, "Someone asked Dalí once, did he use drugs. Dalí said, 'I don't *use* drugs, I *am* drugs.' Art can operate on a lot of levels. Viewers have strong reactions to Sten's work, always have. Fortunately, many of them buy." Her laugh was a secret between them.

"I thought we might talk about last weekend, Mrs. Dymmoch."

"Nola, please."

"Make mine Frank."

"I'm a widow, Frank. I never got used to either of my married names, though mine was a generation eager to take on husbands' identities. Yes, we didn't have much opportunity to talk the other day. I assume you were there because . . . well, *is* something wrong?"

Frank explained what had led him to Utica and now here today. Nola Dymmoch stopped walking. "You really think Herb's crash wasn't an accident?"

"I have to admit the Cooperstown police don't seem too impressed with the idea."

"Did you discover something they didn't?"

"I don't know. I was hoping our talking might focus things. Do you mind?"

"Not at all. No, if it'll help . . ." She studied him from under the brim of her hat.

"I gather from what you said before that you and Frawley weren't close anymore."

"Not for years. God, a lot of them. Do you want to hear all of that?"

He smiled. "It's up to you."

"Well, I first met him when I was at school in Syracuse."

"In kindergarten?"

"God bless you. I was a freshman." She laughed, as if confessing to something. "Ask me what I've done with my B.A. in psych. Herb was playing ball in Utica then, for the Blue Sox. We met on a blind date. He was this rangy, good-looking farm boy from Ohio. I'm a Long Islander. I felt positively worldly compared to him."

"But you clicked."

"Oh, God, no. I could have strangled the friend who'd fixed us up. But Herb was quietly persistent. He'd call from wherever the team was playing, never quite bringing himself to ask for a date, but I could tell he wanted to. Almost as a lark I went with some friends to a night game. I knew nothing about baseball—still don't." She took Frank's arm, balancing as she reached to slip off her sandals. She managed the task with a dancer's grace. Handing the shoes to Frank, she waded into the edge of the sea, where she bent and picked something up. She displayed a small translucent pink shell, which she dropped in Frank's palm, like payment as she took the sandals back.

"I'm a beachcomber. You never know what the tide might bring in."

She left her sandals off as they walked. "Everything about that evening I went to the ball game is as sharp in my memory as a painting—the crisp green field, the white and gray of the uniforms, the aromas, the sounds. Herb was magnificent. To me he was clearly the best player on the field, the most natural. He hit two home runs and made a spectacular catch. That quality of being so good at something, so graceful, won me over. Are you all right? You seem to be limping a little."

Frank didn't want her story interrupted by something so ordinary as his old wound. "I'm okay."

"My house is just down the beach here. We can stop."

"Please go on."

She did, talking about Herb Frawley, describing his childlike excitement at earning his living playing baseball, animated herself in the telling. "We got married the year the Giants called him up to the majors. For a brief time there, I thought we would always be happy." She held her hat in a small gust of sea breeze which teased her hair, wrapped the denim skirt around her well-shaped legs. She reached for Frank's hand. "Come on."

The house was set back among the dunes, starkly modern, yet assimilated by its surroundings. It was weathered a pale silver amid junipers and landscape plantings, with lots of glass giving views across the sands of the outer Cape to the Atlantic. He couldn't imagine such a house being built today; even if land restrictions didn't prevent it, the cost would be prohibitive. Nola offered a cold drink and Frank sat at the center island in the big kitchen while she poured iced herbal tea into tall glasses. An orange tiger cat leaped to the counter.

"Jackson, down!" Nola said.

The cat gave her a jade-eyed stare and paid no attention. "Aggressive and independent," Nola said, "like his namesake."

"Reggie Jackson?"

"Jackson Pollock." She pointed into the large open room beyond, to a painting on the white wall. It looked like a spaghetti spill. "My second husband bought Pollocks early on, when Pollock was just a madman splashing paint on canvas. Before my husband died he sold some of them for twenty times what he'd paid."

"Did your husband own the gallery?"

"Yes. He came from old New York money. He had this place built. We divided our time between here and the South of France."

"Nice. What's that out there?" Frank pointed. Far out on the sand, beyond the big windows, sat an old shack. It was perched near the top of a dune, ringed with wind fences and high grass, and appeared to tilt crazily in several directions at once.

"An old shipwreckers hut, I'm told. There used to be others along the outer Cape. Apparently long ago gangs of thieves would hang lanterns during storms, to fool mariners into thinking there was safe passage. Ships would founder on sandbars out there and break up, the crews get rescued by locals or drown. The wreckers would wait for calmer weather, then go out at night to salvage whatever they could find."

"Sounds like nasty business."

"Later, during Prohibition, that was evidently a bootleggers hut. It's even said to be haunted by the ghost of Eugene O'Neill, who supposedly wrote a play in it."

"Do you believe it?"

"The play part?"

"The ghost part."

"Only when we used to own it." She laughed. "That's national seashore now, so nothing can be touched. It won't last much longer. There's a steep cliff just beyond there, and the beach. The whole outer Cape keeps eroding, year by year. Nauset Lighthouse is almost gone. People talk about California, but I think we'll all drop into the sea sooner."

Frank clinked his glass of tea against hers. "Long life," he said.

Nola resumed talking about her first husband, telling of their early happy years together, moving slowly, inevitably to what changed them.

"Okay, I could appreciate Herb's love of baseball—he was so good at it. But once his career was over, he should have . . ." She didn't complete the thought, staring out toward the sand dunes, and the sea and sky beyond.

"Should have what?" Frank said.

"He should have accepted the fact and gone on to other things."

Frank found the logic of the idea appealing. "What did he do?"

"He tried a few jobs, selling mostly. I think he could have been good at it. People were always willing to like him if he let them. But he could never let go of the past. It used to eat at him. It's at times like that, when façades are taken down, that you see the big spaces between people. We really didn't have much in common. I liked reading and art and travel. I don't think I ever saw him pick up a book. I was struck with all that again at the cemetery the other day." Her voice had grown wistful. "I used to take it for granted that a wife would finally sleep at her husband's side. But I won't." She looked at him. "Are you married, Frank?"

He realized she hadn't said his name before. "No."

He looked for something to add, but he couldn't think of what; then she said, "Our son Jason was a bond for a few years after he was born, but even then there were tensions. Herb tried a comeback, as you probably know."

"I didn't know."

"He played for part of a season in Mexico. It didn't work out. Before the funeral, I hadn't seen Herb in years and years."

"Would he have tried to blackmail anyone?"

The glass stopped at Nola's lips, misted a moment by her breath. Her eyes changed. "Seriously?"

Frank showed her the note he had found in Frawley's room. She said it did look like his writing, but the idea of his sending it to someone . . . "God, I don't think so. Do you?"

He recounted for her what he had learned about the phone call Frawley received at the Birch Bark Lodge.

"And you told the police?"

He had told them very little actually. After finding the note in the beer bottle, he had briefly considered informing Chief Bolick, but he didn't. What would it change? It wasn't really even evidence of anything. "No," he said. "It's nothing they want to know."

She frowned. "Herb's career was brief. I know that ate at him."

"Didn't he consider that having made the show at all meant he was better than ninety-nine percent of the people who ever swung a bat?"

"Maybe it was something else then. I never really understood Herb altogether. All that going from city to city, the training . . . the game absorbed him. But then, I guess I didn't spend a lot of time trying. Of course, you must know that."

He looked at her. Her eyes were miniatures of the dark blue ocean beyond the big windows. "How would I?"

"From Jason. I don't know what he's told you."

"We talked all of a minute. He said he hadn't seen much of Frawley in a long time either."

"And about me?" She gave an uncertain smile. "That sounds vain, I know. I only mean that Jason and I haven't been close for years. He blames me for the fact that he and Herb never really bonded. I think he feels . . . cheated." Frank had not forgotten Jason's abrupt departure at the cemetery. "He's partly justified in being angry," Nola went on. "He was small when Herb and I divorced. I would have agreed to joint custody, but Herb wasn't much interested. So from the age of five until he was in college, Jason had no contact with Herb. He grew to like my second husband, but there was never a real father-son connection."

"Relationships are always tough," Frank said.

"Yes, they are."

"Was there any particular cause why your marriage to Herb ended?"

She looked at him, then away. His was a cop habit, Frank realized: ask the questions quietly but directly. If you overstepped, people let you know one way or another. Usually they answered.

"I've always felt it was tied with his major-league career," Nola said.

"The traveling?"

"Partly that, I suppose, but I used to go with him to spring training. No, I think it was him. After a strong start, I remember that there was a slump that began in his second year."

In 1957. It tallied with the slide in Frawley's statistics, his subsequent departure from the Giants.

"He wasn't the same. He hadn't been injured, or anything. But he just . . . I don't know. Why are you doing this, Frank?"

"I'm sorry, I didn't mean—"

"No, no. Time has healed all that. I just mean . . . you're investing your own time, aren't you? And this happened so long ago. You never knew Herb."

Was it possible he had, in a way? Before he could respond, the telephone rang. Nola took a cordless from a cradle on the counter and spoke a moment, then broke the connection. "That was the gallery. There's a message for you to call your office. Use this if you like." She handed him the phone and went to pour more iced tea.

Gilchrist was at home. "Two things. I made some calls. Both Al Kaline and Jack Livingstone were in Cooperstown for the induction ceremony last weekend. Also, you had a call from Butch Huggins."

"Huggins . . ." Frank tried to place the name.

"The acting fire chief in Cooperstown."

"Right."

"He said tell you he had another look at that car, based on what you'd told him. He said the burn pattern was consistent with a chemical starter splashed on the engine block. He was going to lab test it."

"Really."

"That's not the best part. Best part is this morning he finds out the car's already been sold. It's a three-foot cube of steel at a scrapyard in Albany."

"Nice," Frank said.

"I also had an idea I wanted to lay on you, but I've got another call coming through. Can you hold?"

"I'll get back to you," Frank said. When he hung up, Nola Dymmoch's look was questioning. He told her about Butch Huggins's phone call.

She was thoughtful a moment. "Frank, what if I were to hire you?"

"There's no way of proving now that the car wreck wasn't an accident."

"Couldn't you investigate anyway?"

"I'm licensed in this state, not New York. If I learned anything, we'd have to talk to the state police and the sheriff's office up there. I guess I'd also repeat that without that evidence, and without Chief Bolick's cooperation, it's unlikely we'll have much luck."

"But it's not impossible?"

He shrugged. "I'd like to think that."

"Then, I'd like to hire you."

"Can I ask what you want to gain?" It came out wrong, and he said in a softer tone, "Mrs.—Nola, I'm not the police. This isn't about justice. I look for information."

"That's what I want." She hesitated. "Don't think badly of me, Frank."

The remark put him off stride for a moment, confused him. "I don't. Why would I?"

She gave a sad smile and turned to look out at the dunes. Her profile had kept all of the precise beauty she must have had when she was a young baseball player's wife. "I won't deny it, I didn't put enough into my first marriage. I've got my own sins to atone for, I guess. Herb was an easy man to be tough on. I suppose I feel a small guilt. But in truth, things are almost never one way in life." She turned back, her eyes on his, blue and steady in her middle-aged face. "Herb is dead, and I've accepted that. Jason, however, hasn't. Maybe if he could come to understand more about who his father was, about Herb's life . . . maybe he'd soften his heart. Zoe's parents divorced when she was small. Her mother died, her father she has no contact with—I see the pain that's caused her, being alone. Jason is my only child, Frank. I don't want us to be strangers forever."

10

GILCHRIST SAID, "RIGNEY."

Frank was at a pay phone in North Truro, just outside Provincetown. He had to cover one ear to keep out the noise of afternoon traffic shushing by on 6-A, the narrow stretch of highway between tiny rental cottages, salt marsh, and the great dunes of the outer Cape. "Could you be a little more cryptic?"

"William J. 'Specs' Rigney. Frawley's manager in fifty-seven, and later in sixty-one. I thought he might have some dope on Frawley."

"That was a lot of innings ago. Bill Rigney. Is he even still alive?"

"Was forty minutes ago," Gilchrist said. "That was the call I had coming in. I'd left a message for him. We talked sports half an hour. Dude's cool. Still with the A's organization. He even told me call him collect if I ever spot any hot prospects."

"Spot them doing what? Mugging little old ladies?"

Ever the gentleman, Gilchrist let the crack go. "Your part took three minutes," Gilchrist said, which is what he spent replaying his conversation with the former manager of the Giants and later the original Los Angeles Angels. According to Bill Rigney, by the time Frawley was released by Los Angeles his average had dipped below two hundred and his defensive game had gone south. And his marriage was over, Frank thought.

"He spent the rest of the season at Venice Beach, boozing. Occasionally he'd still show up at the park to talk to Rigney, who was still his mentor. After the season, he went back to Utica, where he had a few homeboys from his Blue Sox days."

"Any names?" Frank asked.

"No. But the questions were all the same, evidently. 'Why? What now? You going to give the game another shot?' In January of sixty-three he began calling his contacts—the first being Bill Rigney—to see if the Angels would give him a tryout. Rigney told him that if it were up to him, he'd have brought Frawley back, even with the cold bat. Guy had been that good. But personnel was the GM's job, and the club had decided to go with youth."

"Frawley would've been . . . what, twenty-eight?"

"Nine. An old man. So anyway, that door swung shut. After that, Rigney lost touch."

"Frawley played a stretch in one of the Mexican leagues," Frank said.

"Okay, you know about that. With the Mexico City Tigers. Any details?"

"No."

"I'll see what I can learn. Meanwhile, who you should talk to, Rigney told me—someone who might've kept in touch—is Floyd Tillman."

Frank didn't have to say anything about being cryptic this time. Tillman was one of the highest-profile sports agents in the country. He handled a constellation of stars from all sports, and was known to make or break deals. "Got his phone number right there, I bet."

"Better than that, but it depends. Are you gainfully employed?"

Frank laughed. "It's official. Nola Dymmoch hired me."

"Good," said Gilchrist. "Money and everything?"

"Yeah."

"Wonderful. I got you a slot in Floyd Tillman's busy calendar. Five-thirty this afternoon. Just show up."

"In New York?"

"Plenty of time. You can be in Hyannis in an hour. There's a two-forty shuttle to Kennedy with lots of seats."

Floyd Tillman's office occupied a suite forty-nine floors above the car-swarmed, honking bustle of Fifth Avenue. Like the August heat, rush-hour chaos was a remote triviality this far up. The atmosphere was of hushed deep carpets, rosewood furniture, potted trees, and the whisper of fax machines delivering important messages. If there was an ideal place to discuss bonuses, multiyear contracts, and sweet endorsement deals, Frank thought, this was it.

He had arrived in the city in time to check into a midtown hotel and put on a fresh shirt and a tie. A receptionist found Frank's name in her appointment book and asked him to have a seat. The walls of the waiting area were decorated with photographs of the agency's household-name clients. Tillman himself appeared in a few of the photos. He didn't get heavier over the years the way Cooperstown police chief Bolick did; he only got older—and happier, if you went by his smile.

Gilchrist's telephone briefing had included the details that Tillman's father, Floyd Sr., had been with the Giants organization both here in New York and after the team defected to San Francisco, so Floyd Jr. had grown up in the game, mostly as a clubhouse rat. Later he had taken a degree in marketing at St. John's. His first clients had been unknowns who had become well-knowns, and he had parlayed those early successes into one of the most powerful agencies around. Now you couldn't turn on TV or the radio without finding one of his athletes hawking this or that.

It was going on six o'clock when the receptionist said, "Mr. Branco, would you come with me?"

She ushered Frank into a conference room where four brown leather chairs were ringed around a gleaming green-marble table. The air was cool and cut with shafts of muted daylight coming through vertical blinds. LeRoy Neiman lithographs adorned the walls. Frank wondered if this was where Michael Jordan had inked his thirty-million-dollar-a-year footwear deal.

"Ah, Mr. Branco." In the recessed lighting, Floyd Tillman's head shone like a maple newel post as he stepped into the room. He was a compact man in an olive-toned suit, with teeth as white as his shirt and a scalp completely shorn of hair. Despite the accoutrements of wealth—the deep tan and smart clothes and the diamond chip that winked from his tie tack—there was still something about him of the clubhouse rat. He had a sly twinkle in his eye, and the look of a man who enjoys a good joke.

"I was delighted when I learned who your associate is," Tillman said, shaking Frank's hand. "What an athlete Ty Gilchrist was. Shame he was cut off in his prime. If he's ever interested in talking, there might be some endorsement work. He uses a wheelchair, doesn't he?"

When they got seated, Tillman played show-and-tell for a moment, displaying a new pair of diamond cuff links he had gotten as a gift from Neon Deion Sanders. Just then a small woman in a beige suit and holding a legal pad came in and took a chair. Did these people coordinate their garb with the furniture? Frank wondered.

"I've asked Ms. Cummings to sit in and take notes." Tillman grinned and winked at Frank. "Of course it means I can't tell any salty stories. Call it a personal quirk, but I keep notes on everything. It's a litigious culture. Coffee or a soft drink?"

Frank declined, and the three of them sat. Tillman expressed regrets over Herb Frawley's death. Since Gilchrist had explained only that the meeting was in regard to a Frawley family matter, Frank decided simply to present himself as working up a profile for the heirs for settling Frawley's estate. The agent seemed satisfied and willing to talk. According to Tillman, Herb Frawley had been a polite and likable athlete. "One time I remember a re-porter asking him, 'How's it feel to be signed by the Giants?' and Herb says—to this day I remember—I was just a kid myself—Herb blushes and says, 'I'm tickled pink.' *Pink.* Hell, these days the game is all green." He shook his head as if it were a mystery be-yond fathoming, or maybe he was thinking of a marketing spin. Then he chuckled. "And next trip to the plate, for his second major-league at bat—against Johnny Sain, it might've been . . . or probably Harvey Haddix, another Ohioan, like Herb—he puts a fastball into the right-field seats. At the Polo Grounds that was a hell of a shot."

There really wasn't a lot that Tillman could say about Herb Frawley. He repeated that he'd been only a boy himself in those days. Frank asked some questions but learned little beyond what he already knew.

"Did Frawley get along well with other players?"

"He had a few friends, but my impression is he mostly kept his mind on his game. He was quiet. He never drew attention ex-cept with his play."

"How was he at the end, when he got cut by the Angels and tried to come back?"

Tillman frowned, as if at a shadow closing in. "After the An-gels took a pass on Herb, he tried San Francisco. The GM at the time was my father. Herb's old roommate, Jack Livingstone, had become the toast of the town out there. And Herb hadn't been pro-ductive in nearly five seasons. He just barely cracked the Mendoza line a couple years there, I think. He was—"

"Sorry?" Ms. Cummings looked up from her pad. "What line was that?"

"Mendoza. You know about that," Tillman said to Frank.

Mario Mendoza, Frank recalled; but he decided to play dumb: Tillman seemed most talkative when he was showing off. "Wasn't he a ballplayer?" Frank asked.

"Played shortstop for Pittsburgh, then a couple other teams. He hung in for eight seasons, just hovering above two hundred, mostly hitting singles. He careered out at two-fifteen or there-abouts." Tillman shook his head. "So the term's come to mean the point where you're just hanging on by the short hairs."

Ms. Cummings went back to jotting.

"Anyhow, that's where Herb was. So when he took a shot at a comeback . . . Well, what could the Giants say?"

The question was rhetorical; both men knew what the Giants had said.

Tillman leaned and spoke quietly to Ms. Cummings, who set her pad down and left the room. When she slipped back in a moment later, she handed him a framed photograph. He looked at it and handed it to Frank. It was a publicity shot. Depicted were two young ballplayers in New York Giants whites, kneeling and holding bats on their shoulders. One was a right-handed hitter, the other a lefty—but the most telling contrast between the two men was in their expressions. Herb Frawley was smiling shyly, his eyes not quite meeting the camera's eye, betraying a kind of bashful tolerance of the occasion. The other man had a direct, confident gaze, and with his deep tan and wide grin, he resembled a young Clark Gable. Tillman anticipated Frank's question. "That's Herbie with Jack Livingstone. That goes back to the beginning. God, talk about a natural."

"Good enough to make the Hall," Frank said.

"Livingstone? He was a schnook—though give him his due, he could play ball. I'm talking Frawley. Herb was born to play ball."

Frank set the photo on the marble table with a soft clack. "Why didn't he, then?"

"Why didn't he?" Tillman leaned back in the leather chair and ran a hand across his shaved scalp. "Why? That question chased around in my mind for years, and I never found an answer I liked. I can picture when he started to go sour. I used to hang around the clubhouse. It was after the Giants broke spring training in fifty-seven and were into the season when things began to unravel. Herb always seemed preoccupied, like something was eating him.

His numbers started to nose-dive. Everyone kept figuring, hey, it's a slump, slumps end. But that one, Christ, I don't know, you know? I mean something like what happened to Ty Gilchrist—a crazy hit by that idiot who blindsided him—at least you can pin the damage on something tangible. But with Herbie . . . it's a mystery. I guess you've just got to be philosophical. Sometimes people have got this tremendous gift, and then they just use it up. Or lose it. Look at Steve Blass. That kid could *throw*. It happens."

Tillman narrowed his gaze, looking at the photograph on the table. "With Herbie it was sad to see. The Giants would've liked to keep him around, but you don't make chicken soup out of chicken shit."

Frank left a card and Ms. Cummings walked him down the deep-carpeted hallway past the smiling photos of big-name sports stars to the elevator.

The restaurant was a narrow cave on West Fifty-seventh Street near Broadway, Greek if you went by the menu and the gimcrack decor, though the waiter greeted Frank in an accent he recognized from spy movies. Jason Frawley appeared five minutes later. He had the same dispirited look he had worn at his father's funeral, but there was a restlessness in his manner too. He was working, he told Frank again, in case Frank hadn't heard it on the telephone. He could take only a short dinner break before he had to get back to his apartment, where he had a home office.

"What is it you do?" Frank asked.

"Computers," Jason said.

It wasn't much of an answer, Frank thought, but anything more would have been wasted on him. They ordered moussaka, and Frank got a carafe of white wine. He poured the wine, taking his time, buttering bread, commenting on the weather and the availability of Manhattan taxicabs, shunting aside Jason Frawley's attempts to direct the conversation. He wanted to slow the rhythm, the way a hitter might alter the pace of a game. Finally, only after the meals had arrived, Frank said, "So, have you thought about what I told you on the phone?"

"First I'd like to know why my mother hired you."

"Partly because she wants a better relationship with you, I gather."

"That's a joke."

Frank shrugged. "Then I'll let the two of you laugh at it. All she's paying me for is some answers about your father's death."

"How do I know that?"

"Because it's all I'll sell."

"And you want me to help you get the answers, to tell you about my father and me."

"That's the idea anyway."

"I hope you didn't come all the way here for that." Jason sighed. "That'll take all of two minutes. My parents split up when I was little, when we were living on the West Coast. He was moving around a lot by then, trying to make a comeback to baseball. After the divorce I didn't see him for probably fifteen years. He'd ended up back in Utica. When I came east for college I looked him up." Jason shrugged, as though that were the whole of it.

Frank refilled the glasses. "What happened then?"

"Is any of this relevant?"

"It might be."

Jason didn't appear convinced. He picked at his food, revealing layers of eggplant and ground lamb, like a surgeon probing a gangrenous wound. "What happened when I saw him . . . well, it was strained. He was a self-contained guy, not real comfortable to be with, not after all those years without any contact between us. But, I don't know . . . in spite of that, I liked him. Even out of shape, the way he was, what with the drinking and lack of exercise, there was a physical quality to him that was exciting to be around. A kind of sureness that people responded to. I wish I'd known him when he was young." He sighed. "I think . . ."

Frank waited, but whatever Jason Frawley was thinking he let go. "Anyhow," he resumed, "we'd get together occasionally, maybe twice a year. The last time I saw him alive was in May."

"In Utica?"

"Here. We went to a Mets game. We never had a lot of common ground. Mainly we talked about the weather, baseball."

It was something a lot of fathers and sons had in common, a kind of male shorthand for emotion. Sometimes it was the only thing, but it was a bond. Between Frank and his own father it had been fishing. Frank said, "Tell me about that last time."

Herb Frawley had phoned out of the blue, said he was in town and would Jason like to go to a game with him. They met at Shea Stadium that afternoon.

"He'd been drinking, but he wasn't drunk. He seemed more animated than usual, like he was keeping a secret. He told me he was going to surprise me, that he was going to get something for me. But he wouldn't say what it was, and that's all I heard about it. And that was the last time I spoke to him in person. In mid-July I got a package in the mail. I tried to phone but didn't reach him. Two weeks later, to the day, I got the call from the police in Cooperstown telling me about the car wreck. I made the funeral arrangements from here."

"Did you speak with your uncle?"

Jason looked puzzled. "Who?"

"The landlady told me your father's brother came by the day after the crash."

Jason Frawley shook his head. "She's mistaken. He doesn't have a brother."

"Brother-in-law?"

"No."

Frank considered that a moment, then went on. "Did you instruct the police not to do an autopsy."

"Yes. What was the point?"

Bolick had been candid about that, at least. "What did your dad send you?"

"His scrapbook."

"Was that the surprise he'd referred to?"

"I don't think so. He'd been telling me for years that he was going to give me the scrapbook. No, I had a sense that he wanted somehow to make up for all that time we'd lost." Jason shrugged. "Of course, maybe I'm imagining it. Other times I don't know if he ever even thought of me at all."

When they walked out into the evening heat, Frank said, "For the record, in his wallet the night he died, your dad had the stubs to that Mets game."

"Yeah? So he hadn't cleaned out his wallet in a while."

"That's one way to see it."

"You have another?"

"Maybe he valued your times together more than he said."

Did Jason stand a little straighter? He stroked his sparse mustache a moment, gazing along the deeply shadowed street, then said, "Would you care to see the scrapbook?"

Jason Frawley's apartment was a one-bedroom on the fifth floor of a modern building on Twenty-seventh Street between Seventh and Eighth, small even for a young bachelor. Without ceremony, Jason brought out the scrapbook, a big brown-covered affair that looked old.

Frank paged through plastic pages containing yellowed newspaper clippings and photographs. Most of the material dated from the late 1950s. One photo showed three young players standing in an outfield by a sign that said 475 feet—which made it the Polo Grounds, where, if Floyd Tillman's memory served, Herb Frawley had put a Harvey Haddix fastball in his second major-league at bat. With the three players was a frizzy-haired man in a suit and fat tie, older by at least a dozen years. They were all smiling for the camera.

"That's Danny O'Connell, the third baseman," Jason said, pointing to the player on the left. "He's dead now. In fact, the only one still alive is Jack Livingstone." Jason pointed at the darkly handsome grinning young man on the right, the Clark Gable look-alike Frank had seen in the photo in Tillman's office. "He and Dad were close. They were roommates Dad's first season."

"Did they stay friends?"

"For a while, but I think they went their separate ways."

Frank indicated the older man in street clothes. "Who's this?"

"Friend of theirs. I don't remember his name. He sold peanuts at the ballpark."

They looked at the other shots, and Frank scanned the newspaper columns, some dating to Herb Frawley's days with the Utica Blue Sox. The young player's talent and promise were evident in the praise the sportswriters had bestowed upon him. There were no pictures in the scrapbook of Nola or Jason Frawley.

When Frank got back to his hotel room, he took off his shoes and shirt and lay on the bed in the dark with the drapes open to the nighttime glow of Manhattan. He let his mind drift. The queen-size mattress was payment for the miles and hours he had traveled. The phone ringing jarred him out of a doze.

"Did I wake you?" Floyd Tillman asked after identifying himself.

"No."

"You stirred up some baseline chalk today, fella. I got to thinking back." Tillman paused. Frank wondered if the call was on a conference line, with Ms. Cummings taking notes, but it seemed late for an office call: 10:27 on the bedside clock.

"Remember I mentioned the Giants nixed the idea of Herbie's coming back? Well, the team had been in San Francisco only a few years then and were working to build a fan base. You know how that goes." Frank knew; put people in the seats. "Anyway, maybe I'm way off, maybe there are ten good sound reasons why they said no—I can think of two right now—but I've got this memory of my father saying that it was a personal thing."

"Personnel?"

"Person*al*. That it was a player who opposed it."

"Who?"

"Jack Livingstone."

Frank had switched on the bedside lamp and was hunting for his notebook. "Could Livingstone do that?"

"He was the draw then, remember. Pulling in those fans. So he had clout with management. My memory is secondhand, from my dad, but I think Livingstone wanted Frawley as far away from Candlestick as possible."

The notebook was on the dresser, across the room. The hell with it. On the carpet, Frank's bare feet had begun to tingle. "Why?"

"You've got me there. They used to be roommates and friends. Of course, my father's been dead twenty years. Who you might talk to, though—and this is why I called—is Lou Lou."

"Who's she?"

"Louis Merloni. He was a vendor at the Polo Grounds. Used to give me free peanuts. If there'd been something going on, Lou Lou would know about it."

On the dresser too was the scrapbook photograph Jason Frawley had loaned Frank: Herb Frawley, Danny O'Connell, Jack Livingstone, and the older man in the fat tie. "Was he a small, wire-haired guy? Big nose?"

"You knew him?"

"I came across a photo."

"Well, he knew more than peanuts, I'll tell you that. Lou Lou was tight with some of the players, including Herb. They hung out together off the field. Like family, practically. He even used to go to Florida for spring training."

"Is he still around?"

Tillman clicked his tongue. "That's anyone's guess. He could be in the graveyard for all I know—he wasn't a young man, even then, but he was a survivor. If I were you, the place I'd try is the card games out at Coney Island. Lou Lou always liked cards, and he was no stranger to the con men out there. But baseball is what he knew best." Tillman laughed. "You find him, tell him I was asking."

11

RAIN FELL OVERNIGHT, AND MORNING CAME IN A SILVER
haze that leveled the city skyline and made Frank squint. He
bought coffee at a deli near the hotel, got some ten-dollar sunglasses from a street hawker who swore they were Ray•Ban, then
took the subway over to Brooklyn. It was ten o'clock when he got
to Coney Island, and the mist was thinning, smudging the line of
honky-tonk amusement rides. So close offshore it hardly seemed
deep enough to bother, a few body surfers were working the soggy
waves. Frank wished he felt as buoyant. After last night's phone
call from Floyd Tillman, he hadn't fallen back to sleep for a long
time. He had awakened this morning with stiffness in his bad leg.
He hoped he wasn't going to have to do a lot of walking.

Beyond Nathan's there were strollers on the boardwalk and
people with fast food and cotton candy drifting into the arcades.
He walked past the photo booths and Skee-Ball and frozen cus-
tard stands. Farther down, several people were gathered around a
young black man on his knees. Frank was too distant to hear words,
but he didn't imagine the young man was a street evangelist. It
seemed like a place to begin.

As Frank joined the outer fringe of onlookers, he heard the familiar pitch, older than Dale Carnegie, and a theme played on by
every huckster of hope since: ten gonna get you twenty.

"Watch the red card," the young man sang, "tell me where it
is. Red card, here we go."

He ran through it a few times, letting himself get caught, bait-
ing the hook. Egged on by her companions, a woman in a brand
new *I Love NY* T-shirt put a twenty-dollar bill on the planks. The
black man did the quick shuffle with the three cards, moving them
around, talking all the while, and let her take it.

"Hey, you quick," he said gamely. "Gon' take all my money.
How 'bout gimme a chance. Double or nothing. You pick the card
you take forty, you don't it's mines."

He lost again. "I gotta practice more," he said.

He was pretty good. Frank watched as other people came;
more money went down. He slid the cards around, moving them
in a showy dance, gold bracelets jingling from thin wrists. When
the ante hit eighty dollars, the kid put his hands on his knees and
stared at the backs of the cards as if he had outsmarted himself.
"Damn," he murmured. "Where's that red at?"

"In your palm," Frank said.

The kid glanced up. What was he, seventeen? With a dark, in-
telligent, angry face. His eyes were on Frank, and in that instant
there may have been a flash of recognition in them. The kid
snatched up the bills, leaving the cards, and sprang to his feet. Darting past the startled tourists, he leaped off the boardwalk to the
beach six feet below.

Let him go, Frank thought. There are others to chase him, or
not, as they choose. Three-card monte wasn't what Floyd Tillman
had meant in directing Frank to the card games. Ah, hell. Frank
used the stairs. He jogged along the mostly empty beach, moving
at a slower speed. He wanted to shout to the kid that he was only
after information, but he saved his breath.

The kid ran under the boardwalk. The damp sand made it hard
to keep up but easy to follow. When Frank reached the place

where the kid had gone, he peered in, but it was like trying to see into a cave. After catching his breath a moment, he pocketed the alleged Ray•Ban sunglasses and stepped in among the ancient pilings.

The splintery underdeck of the boardwalk was just inches above his head. Pigeons or seagull chicks cooed somewhere in the dimness. In here, the light was broken in chips, shafted by the shadows, and the air had a dank taint of iodine, creosote, and urine. Frank went in farther. High tides had brought in seaweed and Styrofoam litter, which crackled underfoot and obscured any trail he might hope to follow. Suddenly the enterprise seemed pointless. He turned to leave, and as he did he saw movement at the edge of his vision: a glint of light on gold, then the flash of steel. He turned abruptly, feeling his bad knee pop. The youth stepped forward with a knife.

Frank raised his hands in an open-palmed gesture of nonaggression and simultaneously stepped sideways, wanting to keep a piling between himself and the knife. The kid moved too, and Frank understood his own vulnerability.

"Big mistake, man," the youth said. "Dissin' me like that."

Frank said nothing, keeping his focus on the kid's body language, the knife in his hand.

"Ax me, man, you shouldn't never have come down here."

At that instant something lashed from the shadows and whacked down on the youth's wrist. Frank jumped back. The knife flew from the kid's hand and imbedded itself in the sand. The kid yelped.

A wooden cane seemed to draw an old man out of the dimness.

"He's a cop!" the youth cried, holding his wrist.

"Shut up, already," commanded the old man. "Back off." The youth did as he was told, sliding behind the old man, who emerged more fully now into a shaft of daylight. He might have been eighty, Frank saw, tall and stooped, with a fresh pink shirt and elastic-waist sport slacks the color of chicken fat. His thin white hair was combed across a bald dome and greased flat.

"Are you?" he asked.

"Private," Frank said.

"You prove it?"

Frank took out his Massachusetts state investigator's license and held it at arm's length. Both the old man and the youth gave it a brief notice.

"Where from?"

"Boston."

The old man motioned with a backward tip of his head. "You got a hassle with him?"

None of the tourists had taken up the chase apparently, or summoned a cop. They were probably heading for the interstate now, or content with the action their money had bought. They could be eating hot dogs, buying T-shirts emblazoned with I GOT TOOK AT CONEY ISLAND. Frank shook his head. "No hassle."

With the tip of his cane, the old man unearthed the knife from the damp sand and scooted it aside. Over his shoulder, he said, "Whaddya want nickel dime, we got real work later. Go on, get cleaned."

The youth bent to recover the knife, but the old man pinned it in place with the cane and the youth ducked back among the pilings and was gone. Frank said, "Doesn't he know dealing crack pays a lot more, with less risk?"

The old man scowled. "I tell him not to waste his time with monte. I pulled him outta Bed-Stuy. He ain't Einstein, but he's smart. I'm working him in."

"I'll bet."

"He could be running with a gang, shooting people. So what's wrong he learns a trade?"

"International Brotherhood of Grifters?"

"It's just a reallocation of resources. Who gets killed? You got a mouth on you. From Boston, huh? It figures."

Frank smiled. He recovered the knife, folded it closed, and handed it to the old man, who dropped it in the pocket of his yellow trousers. "I'm looking for someone," Frank said.

"Like who?"

"Ever hear of a man named Louis Merloni?"

The old man studied Frank a moment. "Come on," he said, "it's damp under here. Buy me a frank."

They used the stairs to the boardwalk and started down it. "Me, I got an excuse," the old man said. "I'm ancient. That limp says chasing perps ain't your specialty no more."

"It never was. I didn't catch your name."

"That's okay, I didn't pay no attention to yours."

They bypassed a string of arcades and souvenir stands to a concession where hot dogs were blistering on a grill, good-smelling on the saltwater air. Frank bought two and they took them in little cardboard troughs and sat on a bench facing the beach. Frank finished his in a few bites, having had nothing but morning coffee. The old man chewed slowly, apparently not in any hurry to get to Louis Merloni, nor anything else for that matter. Down where they had sketched in a court on the damp flat sand, a couple were playing paddle ball, the wooden paddles making a dull *thunk* over the noise from a boom-box radio. Nearby some ragged gulls busied themselves gutting a pizza carton.

"Scenic," Frank said.

The old man grunted. "Imagine how beautiful this must've been a hundred years ago. Y'know what always ruins a good thing? Transportation. It brings in people like me. And my father before me. He wasn't two years out of the shtetl near Kraków, and he's out here making a good buck working a speakeasy owned by Murder, Inc. The nineteen-twenties this was. Along here was all big amusement parks, and the people would troop over from the city with the kids and the food. The Newport of the Poor they used to call this. They'd come over in bundles on the subway, looking for cheap thrills. Gambling wasn't legal, and the girlie shows had been cleaned out, so there were card games. I started playing when I was twelve years. It was a happening place." He waved a hand. "Gone. I remember the night in forty-four when Luna Park burned to cinders."

He stopped talking to finish eating. When he had fastidiously wiped his fingers on a handkerchief, and dabbed mustard off his yellow trousers, he said, "The first mistake a mark makes is thinking he's smart. He figures he can see quicker than the next guy."

Frank considered this a moment, trying to foresee where it was going, but he couldn't. "What's his second?"

"Faith in his fellow man. He still thinks life is on the level. Those two together keep him where he is." The old man clapped his hands on his thighs and rose creakily. Frank stood too, moving to keep up as the man began to walk. "Lou Lou Merloni, now there's a name to conjure with. What's he done? Though if you're private, it's probably something he *hasn't*. He owe someone money?"

"I want to ask him about a ballplayer he knew."

"A ballplayer? From when he was pushing goobers at the Polo Grounds?"

"From then."

The leathery face asked the next question with its creases.

"Herb Frawley," Frank said.

"Oh, him."

"You knew him?"

The old man quelled a belch. "Joe DiMaggio I heard of. Jackie Robinson. Baseball ain't my game. I ain't seen Lou Lou in must be five-six years. Not since he saw the light."

"What light was that?"

"Took Jesus Christ as his personal savior is the way I remember him telling it. Saw the error of his wayward ways." The old man stopped at the railing and looked at the beach, where some college-age kids in city T-shirts were spearing litter with spiked sticks. "Lou Lou was living with his daughter or his niece, down Asbury Park way."

"Where Springsteen used to play?"

"Who?"

"Never mind. Go ahead."

"I told you, baseball I don't follow." The old man started to walk again. "Lou Lou though, he loved the game, liked palling around with the players, talking big, spending dough. After the Giants moved out west, he kind of lost purpose. He worked over at Yankee Stadium a lot more years, and would come out here some, but it wasn't the same for him. Maybe that's why he found religion. Maybe it gave him the feeling of being part of something big again. He was like an older brother to those ballplayers."

"Is he still in Asbury Park?"

"Actually it was the town next door there, Ocean-something. They got this old-timey summer camp meeting thing—stomp your feet, say amen. If he hasn't been bitten handling poison snakes or struck dead by lightning, Lou Lou might be there."

"Five years ago you said."

"Or whatever. At our age, his and mine, that's like that." His fingers made a soft dry *snap*. He didn't bother to quell the belch this time, and Frank was gifted with the aroma of spiced meat.

12

THE GARDEN STATE PARKWAY WAS MIRAGES AND TOLL
booths and the whisper of the car radio as Frank drove south in a
rented Ford. He found a jazz and blues station out of Newark that
lasted awhile, and by the time he had exited and headed toward
the Shore, the sun had made a return. It was shining brightly when
he reached the tree-lined center of Ocean Grove. The main street
consisted of small, family-owned businesses and several cozy
restaurants, in one of which he drank coffee and read a brochure
provided by the local tourist information bureau. This had to be
the town that the old grifter at Coney Island had been referring to.

Founded in 1869, Ocean Grove had been established as a
Methodist summer resort, a place (according to one early claim)
"free from the dissipations and follies of fashionable watering
places." It had kept much of its original charm, especially in the
Victorian gingerbread cottages nestled amid groves of pines. And
it was still very much a Christian retreat. The center of life here,
Frank quickly learned, was the Great Auditorium, a ten-thousand-
seat tabernacle which hosted gospel concerts and revival services,

and was now in high season. The waitress smiled when she left the check. "God loves you," she said.

The tabernacle parking lot was busy with cars, some kind of Saturday service just ending. People were departing from the large wooden building in clusters, talking quietly. Walking among them Frank felt rough, his broken nose a badge of his outsider status, though except for an occasional nod of greeting, no one paid him any attention. As he entered the auditorium, he nearly collided with a black man carrying a yellow bucket heaped with checks and large-denomination currency. For an instant, Frank wondered if the man was stealing it. A reverse of the thought seemed to occur simultaneously to the man, who eyed Frank guardedly. Then both relaxed.

"I'm looking for a man named Louis Merloni," Frank said.

The man played with the name awhile before shaking his head and directing Frank toward some people standing together in the aisle at the front of the hall. The group consisted of a man and four well-dressed women, all long into their retirement years. They turned at Frank's approach. He asked his question. There were puzzled looks, a shaking of heads; then one of the women, who wore a brittle silver bouffant, said, "Oh, wait. Merloni. Wasn't that Jane Syrk's mother's maiden name?"

"Of course," said a thin woman with small even teeth. She reminded Frank of Nancy Reagan. "I remember him now. You must mean Jane's uncle."

"Is he around?" Frank asked.

The gentleman excused himself. "We'll see you at prayer meeting, Randolph," the woman with the bouffant said. "Bye, Randolph," the others called. Randolph smiled at Frank, nodded, and left. "His wife passed away last year," volunteered the Nancy Reagan double.

"Louis Merloni's?" Frank asked.

"Randolph's."

"We're all widows," said a third woman.

Frank didn't know what to say to that, so he merely nodded gravely, though none of the widows seemed gloomy.

"In answer to your question, young man, Jane's uncle isn't here anymore. I believe he had a heart attack."

"Yes, he did."

"He's gone too, then?" Frank said.

"Oh, I don't think so. You'd need to talk with Jane," the widow with the bouffant advised.

Jane Syrk, it turned out, *was* in Ocean Grove. The women walked outside with Frank and as a group gave directions to where Lou Lou Merloni's niece rented one of the tiny cottages. He thanked them and they told him he was welcome to join the community for potluck at two o'clock. "There'll be baked chicken and corn, and some wonderful preaching."

And Randolph? Frank wondered. They all smiled and said good-bye.

The cottage was one of many on a narrow, shady lane, distinguished from its neighbors by the Chinese red gingerbread trim. All of the cottages had seen decades of coastal weather. Beside the screen door was a tole-painted sign in the shape of a heart that said WILLKOMMEN. A short woman answered his knock. She appeared to be about Frank's age, with a plain, unadorned look. "Mrs. Syrk?"

"It's *Miss*, actually." Her smile said she wasn't offended, and revealed a small, provocative gap between her front teeth.

"My name is Frank Branco."

"Hi there." She wore a pale yellow sundress buttoned to the collar, her brown hair loose and full. Despite her efforts at plainness, there was a subdued feminine charge that came through.

"I wonder if I could have a word with you," Frank said.

"Are you the Collyers' friend?"

"No. I wanted to talk about your uncle."

Jane Syrk stared at him, and for a moment it was as if the good cheer had been airbrushed away, leaving a vacancy. Her hand rose slowly to her mouth. "Oh, no. Something's happened. Is he gone?"

Frank said that's what he had come to ask her. He quickly gave her a card. There was a bewildered moment as she looked at it, then at him. "You're not from Eventide, then."

"Where's that?"

"And you don't know the Collyers?"

He revealed how he had gotten her name and address. They were still standing in the open door. Jane Syrk stepped back. "Why don't you come in."

The house seemed more spacious than it appeared on the outside, full of light. It had white curtains, hard-scrubbed pine floors and furniture, and the seasonal smell that places which are boarded up much of the year have. A shelf of Reader's Digest condensed books stood above an upright piano that had been painted blue and decorated with birds. The sheet music on it looked like gospel songs.

"Sit down," Jane Syrk invited.

Frank selected a sofa with crocheted doilies on the armrests that seemed to beg for gentleness, and explained more fully what had brought him.

"Ah, well, my uncle did have a heart attack several years ago, though not a severe one," Jane Syrk revealed. "And you think he could help with what you're investigating?"

"He used to be close with Herb Frawley, apparently. It's possible he might remember something that would be helpful."

"You understand that my uncle hasn't had any contact with all of that for a long, long time. He's been in a nursing home in Florida for the past three years. His mind isn't what it was. All that was so long ago."

"So he's . . ." Frank caught himself before saying *senile*.

Jane Syrk smiled. "No longer lucid? The surprising thing is that he is. He's really quite sharp at times. But at other times . . . you're right."

"Ms. Syrk, I wouldn't impose if there weren't the possibility of a crime having been committed."

"I see. Well, I really don't know. My mother was his kid sister. He never married. I'm his only living kin. There's no way I can answer right out—and yet certainly I'd like to help right a wrong." She watched him a moment, her eyes seeming to search for something; then she said, "I'd have to pray about this and get back to you."

It seemed the best offer he was going to get. "When would that be?"

Jane Syrk gave her attractive smile, with its distinctive gap. "In God's time, Mr. Branco. I leave everything to him. But it could be soon. Are you going to the cookout?"

Corn and chicken and good preaching too? "Yes, I am," he said.

The cookout was a homey affair, held in a clearing beside a grove of pines: straw picnic hampers and gingham tablecloths and lots of food and lemonade. Younger people pitched horseshoes. Randolph was there, ringed with women, his plate covered only with green salad, Frank noted. He wasn't going to jeopardize the bounty of this late harvest by plugging any more arteries than he could help. There was some singing, and a bald man in an apricot-colored blazer over brand-new blue jeans spoke about the "therapeutic community of believers." Frank was talking to a retired gym teacher from Virginia Beach who knew her sports and, when she learned he was from Boston, expressed an intense interest in the Red Sox. Jane Syrk appeared. "Here you are," she greeted Frank. "Hi, Helen."

Frank tried to gauge from her expression if she'd been praying. The gym teacher, Helen, looked a little resentful as she excused herself.

"I've thought about what you asked me," Jane said. "Perhaps we can help each other."

"All right. I'm game."

"We need to talk first."

They walked away from the others, into the pine grove. The carpet of needles was spongy underfoot, the air fragrant with the smells of cooking and the ocean. Jane Syrk stopped and looked at him. In the outdoor light, time's abrasions were there in her face: a hint of hard living that was out of phase with her bright demeanor. "The truth is . . . I'm desperate," she said. "I've tried everything. A healing service, laying on of hands, the unceasing prayers of the faithful . . . but so far my uncle hasn't yielded."

"In what way?"

"Five years ago he went forward at a revival service, right here in Ocean Grove. But that was before his heart attack, and being confined in the nursing home. It's nice there in Sarasota, comfortable and all, and his physical needs are met . . . but being laid up has idled his mind, and I'm afraid he's regressed, mentally and spiritually. He's backslidden." She paused. "Frank, I don't have to tell you this, I suppose. It's not really related—but I want to."

"All right," Frank said.

"Before I got saved . . . I lived a life I wish I hadn't." Jane Syrk's voice had lowered and taken on a note of suppressed excitement. From the clearing beyond the trees came the clang of a horseshoe hitting the stake. "I fell in with the wrong people and before I knew it, I was hooked on drugs. I was a prostitute in New York City. I made some dirty movies." She drew a breath and went on. "But that changed at a prayer meeting in Harlem. I went forward and got saved. I'm different now. I'm clean and I'm productive and I'm happy. Praise God. But my old lifestyle . . . it caused a lot of distance and pain between my uncle and me. On both sides. It's . . . complicated. I've tried to make up for that lost time. Uncle Lou and I have built a relationship, and I want us to let go of our old pains. I want him to be at peace too. You, Frank—you may be an answer to prayer. If you'd be willing to go see him . . ."

"In Florida?"

"It can't be done by telephone. He often doesn't even know *me* on the phone. But in person he can be very lucid. Perhaps he could help you with what you want to know."

"You said he's in a nursing home."

"Eventide Senior Care, yes. In Sarasota." She paused and dropped her eyes. For a moment she kicked lightly at a pinecone. With her face lowered, he could see the young woman she had been: pretty and vulnerable, and people had taken advantage of that. But there was strength there too, and she had risen from where she had been. She met his eyes. "Frank," she said with a soft intensity, "I want my uncle slain."

He stared at her.

She nodded eagerly. "You might be the means to do it."

He didn't move. "You want your uncle murdered?"

"*What?*" There was a silence, then Jane Syrk laughed. It made a bright sound there among the pines, like the ringing of horseshoes. "Oh, goodness. It's an expression. 'Slain in the spirit.' It means sanctified . . . obedient to *His* will."

Frank laughed too.

"My uncle may not live much longer. I want him to be at peace."

"I'm no evangelist," Frank said.

"Uncle Lou used to love baseball. The game was his passion. I remember when he'd visit us, when I was small. He'd always bring peanuts, the kind that were salted in the shell. He'd talk about the action, the players he knew—maybe even the man you're interested in. It was so exciting to hear him. But no earthly passion, or excitement, is ever enough when it comes to final things. I know that. Still, it's possible that some contact with that past might spark his interest again . . . draw him out of himself, get him to see life has meaning. And maybe he could help you too. We'd all be blessed. I'm excited this opportunity has come along. I've prayed for it, Frank. It's like a little window that God has opened just a crack."

Jane gripped his hand, her eyes shining. "Praise the Lord," she said.

Frank could think of nothing else to say, so he said, "Amen."

13

Frank picked up his car at the airport in Hyannis at
7:30 that evening and made a phone call to the Dymmoch Gallery
in Provincetown. Nola Dymmoch sounded excited to hear from
him. She said if he hadn't eaten dinner yet why didn't he drive out
and join her. The idea of seeing her appealed to him, and he accepted.

"I'm dying to know what you've found out," Nola said.

"It isn't much, I'm afraid."

"I'll wait till I see you, then."

He telephoned Gilchrist in Boston.

"Religious colony to an old folks home way down south."
Gilchrist's tone was musing when Frank had filled him in. "Interesting line of detection."

"That sounds like faint praise."

"Have you listened to the rap you just laid on me? Man, I hope
the nice lady you've got paying you isn't on a tight budget. A pre-
historic peanut vendor and his jazzed-on-Jesus niece?"

It *was* a long shot. Still, Lou Lou Merloni was the best lead
Frank had at the moment. "I didn't say I'm going to Florida. Nola

Dymmoch calls the shots. But what about you? Learn anything?"

"Negative on Al Kaline. He was supposed to be in Cooperstown for induction weekend, but he had to cancel. Jack Livingstone was there, though. He's on tour."

"Doing what?"

"Writing his name. Puts it right there in the sweet spot—that little place on a baseball where the stitching arcs together? Thirty-five bucks, thank you very much."

Evening traffic was light: summer people out cruising for fried clams, ice cream, and miniature golf. Frank tuned in the ball game and listened to the Sox draw even from a two-run deficit. He was in P-town in fifty minutes.

The Dymmoch Gallery on Commercial Street was closed, but Zoe, Nola's assistant, greeted Frank and let him in. She was garbed in her trademark black, the purple streak vivid in her dark hair under the track lights. "Nola just stepped out for a minute. I'm working on the Nordgren exhibit."

It was scheduled to open in a few days. The artist was going to attend, which had Zoe excited. Despite her gothic look, she seemed giddy as a schoolgirl as she talked of Sten Nordgren and his work. More of the paintings had been hung, the installation nearly complete. Considering several of the large, blurry-faced nudes, Frank was struck again by their stark eroticism.

"Where's the dividing line between what gets hung here and what you might find in a skin magazine?"

Zoe's glare said such philistinism was beneath her contempt.

"The question's innocent," Frank insisted. It had long seemed to him that the contemporary scene was more about getting a group of people to put a price on something than about talent or value, though he admitted his ignorance of art.

Zoe took up the gauntlet. She talked about art's search for new metaphors and images. "Sure, the roles of the critic and the exhibitor are crucial—ab ex needed Betty Parson in its early days—but the work comes first. Without that, nothing else exists. Sex and violence—nudity, pain, death—those've been elements of painting since the beginning. But Nordgren puts them out front." She indicated several of the bolder canvases to make her point. "He's part of tradition, but he isn't bound by it. The blurred faces suggest the ultimate mystery of the human individual, even to ourselves. Primitive man was humble enough to admit his ignorance, which opened him to reverence. In our century we've grown arrogant."

"And irreverent," Frank said.

"If the label fits." Zoe's look was defiant.

Nola had returned during the tail end of the discussion, and came over now smiling. "This sounds high-level."

Frank shook her hand. "Zoe's giving me an art lesson. I'm a slow learner, but I have to confess, you make some good points. I've got things to think about now." He held out his hand to Zoe too, and she shook it, grinning for the first time.

Nola invited her to join them for dinner, but Zoe said she wanted to stay and work while her energy was flowing. Nola and Frank strolled out into the gauzy summer dusk.

"That was noble of you," Nola said playfully. "Were you really convinced?"

"It was a tactical retreat, but she did score points. I'm out of my element, though. It took me a while to realize ab ex isn't a laundry detergent. It's abstract expressionism, right?"

"Bravo. But seriously, I'm glad you engaged her. You forced her to respond. Zoe's full of *feelings* about life, but she has difficulty articulating them. She's a lonely young woman. She needs to get out of herself more."

"She gets pretty worked up over this Nordgren."

"She's been a little in awe of Sten's work since she discovered it here last summer. She can't wait to meet him. I'm not so sure about it, myself."

"No?"

P-town's narrow, winding streets were full of people, penetrated only here and there by a motorist patient or brazen enough to deal with the crowds. Frank was aware that Nola had moved closer to him, talking in a softened voice. "Zoe's vulnerable to ideas. Nordgren has got a very dark vein to his work. He grew up in Europe at the end of the war—he thinks we Americans are naive, overly optimistic."

"That old rap?"

"I know. He's lived in the States for decades; he's just convinced we haven't fully come of age yet, haven't acknowledged our dark side. Zoe's taken by that idea. You ought to hear some of the music she's into. God, talk about bleak!"

"Do I hear your college psych degree working?" Frank said.

She laughed. "Jung. It's a persuasive idea—that we all have a shadow side, that there's health in recognizing it, losing some of our innocence. Nordgren takes it further though. He believes that under the veneer everyone is capable of ... terrible things. Grotesque acts." She slowed her pace and looked at Frank. "Do you agree?"

He could see how such a belief might grow in someone who'd seen war firsthand, who'd paid close attention to much of the twentieth century. The thought had occasionally rasped across his own mind when he'd worked as a city cop. Nola was watching him, the good humor gone from her eyes, replaced with a taut expectancy. People flowed past them in the night-lit street. "Not entirely," he said. "Not everyone."

He was prepared to explain, but she took his arm and said quickly, "Neither do I." As they moved on, he had the feeling he had passed some kind of small test.

They ate in a small shellfish bar on the backside of the Pilgrim Monument—one of P-town's best-kept local secrets, Nola said. During the meal he replayed his conversations with Floyd Tillman, the old con man at Coney Island, and Lou Lou Merloni's niece in Ocean Grove. Nola was particularly interested in his meeting with her son, Jason. When they'd finished eating she said why didn't they go back to her house for a drink.

They retrieved his car, and Frank drove out a slender spit of land. It was away from downtown, an undeveloped stretch with water on both sides of the paved road. Her house was at the end. In the dark, with light glowing through skylights and big windows, it seemed even larger than it had the other day. Inside Nola fixed him a scotch and soda; she stayed with iced tea, and they went out on the deck. The night was windless, starlit over the black shimmer of dunes and the Atlantic. As Frank settled in a wooden deck chair, Jackson Pollock, the big tiger cat, came majestically out and sat at his feet and watched him. After a moment, it leaped softly into Frank's lap and lay down.

"Jackson," Nola said.

"He's all right."

The cat began to purr, and Nola returned to the topic of Jason. She was interested in his final meeting with his father, in May at a Mets game. "And Herb seemed secretive and told Jason he was going to give him something valuable," she mused.

"Mean anything?"

"Not really. I don't know what Herb had to give. Unless he has a deposit box hidden away somewhere. But you didn't find any evidence of that in his room in Utica . . ."

"No."

She nodded. "In the days when Herb played in the major leagues, there wasn't a very big pension. Not by any modern standard."

"How were the funeral expenses covered?"

Nola shrugged. "Jason made the arrangements; I paid for them. I retained a local attorney up there to oversee probate, and to handle any claim the home owners might bring on account of the crash. There's a small savings account, but it'll be some time before his estate is cleared. What else did they talk about?"

"Baseball."

"Could Herb simply have meant the scrapbook?"

"Jason says no. He believes Herb intended for him to have that all along."

They sat quietly, Nola looking out over the dark hills of sand, Frank stroking the orange cat. The silence felt like an accusation for the skimpiness of what he had learned; and it *was* skimpy. Still, he could not let go of the idea that Herb Frawley's death was not what it seemed, that it was tied in some way to his past. In part to suppress his own uncertainty, he replayed for Nola his reasons, beginning with Frawley's driving to Cooperstown on a suspended license, the phone call at the Birch Bark Lodge, after which he had left—sober, according to the woman working the bar. And there was the old scorecard, and the note Frank had found in Frawley's room.

"It's possible that what Herb planned to give Jason was the money from a blackmail scheme."

"That just doesn't sound like Herb," Nola said.

"Though you said you haven't been in touch with him in years."

"That's true . . . but you feel you *know* people, understand what they're capable of. Still . . ." She let the thought fade. "So let's say this Merloni person in the retirement home is the best lead we have—it's pretty speculative."

"I know," Frank admitted. "And that was a long time ago. It's probably a waste of money."

"No, I didn't mean that. It's just that Florida . . . well, you know, it brings back the times I was there with Herb."

He'd upset her, Frank thought. He hadn't meant to. "So maybe we should let it go."

"Is that what you want to do?"

"That's really up to you," he said.

"Advise me, Frank. You don't want to stop. Why?"

Admittedly, he wasn't eager for the swelter of Gulf Coast summer, but the inkling was there that he had invented connections, imagined a crime where none existed. Why, indeed? To occupy old skills? To be busy? Gilchrist had seen the possibility already. Or did it go deeper than that, to some place where Frank wanted to grapple with Herb Frawley's failure in order to better understand his own? He pushed away these thoughts. No, the reason was instinct, a gut feeling that something wasn't right. Still, he thought of the old notion—Chinese, maybe—that if you saved a person's life, you were responsible for it. But what if in *failing* to save the life, you were responsible in another way?

"I don't know, I—" He faltered. He felt on the brink of telling her about Maximo Diaz, but he didn't, and then the telephone rang.

Nola went into the house. She was gone for a while. Jackson, nestling in Frank's lap, had become a warm pressure, recalling in him some need which hadn't died with his injury, or with Kate's leaving. When Nola returned, she was wearing a pale green nylon running suit. "That was Zoe, saying she's locking up and going home."

"Yeah, well," he said, setting the cat on the deck. "It's late."

"Frank, I don't understand the game." Her words stayed him in the chair.

"Game?"

"Baseball. I'm not a fan. You are though. An athlete. I can tell. Were you a boxer?"

Frank mastered an impulse to touch his nose. "Just careless one time."

Her eyes were bright, picking up a glow from inside the house, giving him her young profile. She hadn't sat down again. The lightweight nylon of the running suit rustled softly. "It makes you look competent."

He laughed. "It probably means just the opposite."

"No. You're someone who stands up to things. *For* things. I feel that. I like it. Come on." She held out a hand to him. He let Nola pull him to his feet.

She went down the steps and Frank followed. On the sand she set off in a run. Awkwardly, having sat too long, he jogged after her. They went along the base of the dunes, moving on a kind of natural trail amid the grasses. Off to the right, atop the highest dunes, visible in tilting silhouette against the starlight, sat the abandoned shipwreckers shack where Eugene O'Neill's ghost was said to live. Nola ran down a sandy trace, with Frank slowly following, to the beach far below.

The sea was a vast, calm darkness, pricked here and there with starlight or what might have been passing ships. At its edge Nola slipped off the pants of the sweat suit, then the jacket, and dropped both on the sand. Underneath she wore a slim, two-piece bathing suit, dark against her skin. Frank was huffing when he caught up. Nola waded into the ocean and dove under. She surfaced and without turning to look back started out with a strong, smooth crawl. He watched a moment, then began unbuttoning his shirt. Briefly, when he'd got his shoes and slacks off, he wondered if he should leave his underpants on, but it seemed a needless propriety on the empty beach, so he drew them off. Hard-muscled and pale, he stepped into the foaming surf. Soon he was following Nola Dymmoch again.

He swam easily, and was reminded that the sea was the one place where his bad leg was no liability. It was why underwater recovery work for the cops had absorbed him for a time, made him feel he could still contribute; but it was a random skill, called for only occasionally. Life was lived upright, on land. He dug his cupped hands deeper. He reached Nola's side, and together they continued to swim out. When they were a hundred yards offshore, they stopped and trod water and caught their breath.

"It's lovely," Nola said.

"Warm," he agreed.

She swished her hand and it made a glittery arc in the water. He did it too, and got the same effect.

"Magic," he said.

"The Gulf Stream is close this year. It's bioluminescent plankton."

"I figured as much," he said, and laughed.

She laughed too. "In the tropics I've seen it glow for miles in the wake of ships."

He liked that in her. She possessed a quick awareness of the world around her, and it seemed to expand his. How old was she? Fifty-three? More? He didn't know. She had run like thirty in the dunes, and she swam like twenty. He realized he didn't care, it didn't matter.

The sky overhead was a mirror image of the sea, lucent with stars. They lay there, floating. Nola said, "I remember as a child lying under the rear window of my parents' car when we'd be driving at night. I'd watch the heavens and imagine I was an explorer, moving toward the stars in my spaceship. It seems possible again when I come out here at night by myself."

He lifted his head. "You do this alone?"

"Not often. When I'm feeling brave. I like it with you here."

He liked it too. He felt good, felt a body awareness of her there a few feet away that stirred him. If the warm sea had let him forget his nakedness, he was reminded of it now. Their fingers brushed as they trod water, and the sea sparked. When his hand touched her arm she didn't flinch away. He lifted his head from the water and her face was a foot away from his. She was looking at him with a gaze so intent he wanted to say something to break it, but he didn't know what to say. He reached for her hand, but she had turned and begun swimming toward shore.

She was in chest-deep water, waiting, when he got there. She thumbed her hair back and with the motion of lifting her elbows revealed that she had shed the top of her swimsuit. Her breasts gleamed, darkening the tan around them, the gentle rise and fall of the ocean cupping them. Drawn, as if by something tidal, he moved to her.

"Frank," she whispered, and he kissed her.

Her mouth tasted of the sea. Her hands went down his back, making the muscles clench, and drew him close as he drew her. He had risen to erection. She moved back and unclipped a side clasp, and her bathing suit bottom came away. She flung it toward the beach. He lifted her, settling her legs around his hips. She was light, buoyant in the low waves, and it was as if their bodies ran together, concealed in the sea. He could not have said for sure where one of them ended and the other began. With the ocean sparkling around them, they rode the slow rhythm of the swells.

Hours later he woke in the dark and for half a breath he did not know where he was; then he did. A delicate tinkling sound had invaded his dream. Nola was gone from her side of the big brass-and-iron frame bed. He drew off the flowered comforter, got up, and pulled on his pants. Barefoot, he padded through the house. Downstairs, the curtains in the open doorway to the deck were stirring. Beyond them, wind chimes tinkled. Nola was leaning on the outer railing, wrapped in a bright Navajo blanket, gazing out toward the dunes. He joined her at the rail. "Couldn't sleep?"

"I didn't want to," she said. "The surf has come up. Hear it?"

He could. It rumbled a long way off, a basso profundo to the high night music of the wind chimes. Nola drew in a breath and let it out with a sigh, and only then did he notice that the air had cooled. His torso was prickled with gooseflesh.

"Here, get under here," Nola invited, extending part of the blanket like a large wing. He moved in close to her. She said, "I used to imagine that time was like water. That it could be damned up somehow and captured. I exercise every day. I swim, I run on the beach, I do yoga. I'm careful of what I eat. But I wonder . . ." She turned to look up at him. "What am I saving myself for?"

He had no answer. He felt the attraction again, more strongly than before, deeper, and running both ways. She slid her arm through his and, half turning, murmured, "Maybe it's time to begin spending."

At that moment he felt all hesitation vanish. There was no need for an answer; *how?* and *why?* had been circumvented by the simple force of gravity. He put his arms around her, and she snuggled warm against his chest, the rough wool blanket around them both. Her hair had a scent of rose petals and the ocean. "Go," she breathed. "Please go."

"What?"

"Those first few years with Herb . . . there was an energy flowing for him that was pouring right back into us. A man hitting home runs on the diamond is hitting them at home too. Then it stopped." She put fingers on Frank's lips, forestalling any response he might make, though none had occurred to him except to kiss the fingers. "It stopped at the same time as his slump began," Nola said. "Maybe they're linked. Go to Florida, Frank. Go talk to that old man. I want you to find the truth."

14

On Monday, August 9, in the company with one hundred strangers, Frank came soaring down out of the sky into the lights and sunset murk of a Florida Gulf Coast evening. What had been a little puddle-jump airport when he had visited Sarasota long years ago had grown into a busy operation: food and drink and souvenirs, nonstop service from Boston, and lots of tourist accents on the bustling travelers. He rented a car and made his way out Route 10, into the city. The evening heat was palpable, and although the traffic wasn't the sluggish river of cars one would find during high season, he couldn't help wishing that Herb Frawley had managed to meet his end in a cold January. But he felt like a man on a quest, with a lady waiting for him. That was the surprise. Last night the how and why of her attraction had been shunted aside, but today, given the time he had had on the flight down to mull it, he had probed. And come to what conclusion? Only this: that they were attracted to each other. Excessive analysis was a young lover's mistake, as Kate had often tried to persuade him. Romance was an experience, not a mystery in need of solution. It was a good feeling; that much he knew.

He chose a motel near the beach, part of a durable chain operation, a U-shaped affair, two floors, off-season rates, pool in the courtyard, lounge attached, room with a view of the parking lot and his rental Ford, egg yellow in the gleam of bug lights. As he settled in, unwinding, he discovered a desire to call Nola in Provincetown. And say what? Share with her the trivia of his day? The drive back up to Boston after their breakfast together, his visit with Gilchrist, suitcase packing, airport delays, the sudden swim of panic when the plane had hit turbulence over the Carolinas, and now this: AC chill, standard fire-retardant aromas of carpet, bedspread, and drapes, the pebbled-glass lamp slung from a chain over the Formica table, pay-per-view TV? Or should he confess to her how much of this work was instinct, intuition, hunch? Having been a cop, he understood the distinctions; but now, working as a licensed day laborer, without city resources, you acted quickly, sometimes leaping before you'd fairly looked—and in the present instance, that was entirely possible. But fifteen hundred miles was a long distance across which to voice doubts. He resisted the phone call and settled instead on laps in the night-lit pool, some stretching exercises for his bad leg, and then—why not?—a round of push-ups and sit-ups. And afterward, in the motel lounge, with a flagon of beer, he examined himself in the back-bar mirror and was forced to smile with a sudden awareness: he had wanted to call Nola for no other reason than to hear her voice.

Early the next morning, having breakfasted on a bagel and black coffee, he set out through off-season Sarasota. He brought along a big brown envelope containing his notebook and the old Polo Grounds photograph Jason Frawley had loaned him: Herb Frawley, Jack Livingstone, Danny O'Connell, and Lou Lou Merloni. Orienting from a map the motel had supplied, useful mostly for pinpointing other outlets of the chain around South Florida, he located the Eventide Senior Care Center. It was as Jane Syrk had described it: a low, functional stucco building bleached white by the sun, set on a parched square of lawn ringed with clumps of well-groomed palmetto. He found the visitors' parking area and eased the rented car in amid chair vans and Cadillacs.

In the lobby, a pale black nurse was being yelled at by an ancient fellow in a wheelchair and a VFW cap. The nurse stood there, "yes, sirring" patiently. Finally the old soldier saluted, executed an about-face, and wheeled off into the sunshot corridor. Seeing Frank, the nurse managed a smile. "Mr. Krupner's off his meds again. Help you?"

At Frank's introduction, the nurse said she was the shift supervisor, Barb Wackowski. There seemed to be a sparkle of mirth in declaring the Polish name. She said that Jane Syrk had phoned ahead to say that her uncle could expect the visit. Mr. Merloni was just finishing his hydrotherapy, but if Frank wanted to chat, she was about to go for a smoke. He accompanied her out to an enclosed porch with lounge chairs and Casablanca fans. He declined a cigarette.

"I've mostly quit," Nurse Wackowski said, lighting up, "but I have my days. Being around these people reminds me the clock is always ticking."

"Grab it while you can?"

"That's the idea anyway." She grinned.

"Does Mr. Merloni get many visitors?" Frank asked.

"Only his niece, when she comes down a couple times a year. She's a peach, really, but I think she expects there's a balm in Gilead. She's looking for a miracle for the old guy."

"She's very religious," Frank said noncommittally.

"It's cool with me. You're talking to an Alabama Baptist preacher's daughter here. Mr. Merloni has got no other family, and he's outlived his friends, apparently. Which is why he's here." She gave a smoky sigh. "It's frustrating at times, all these old folks, none of them natives. They gave their productive, energetic years to Michigan, Connecticut, Ohio, Maine—anyplace but here. But when they're old and spent and ready to die . . . not complaining, mind you. The work's fulfilling, and the money piles up if you let it." She laughed. "I'll get the hang of that last part one of these days. So, what would you like to know?"

"Is Lou Lou Merloni dying?"

"Lou Lou. *That's* what he said they used to call him. Dying? Not in any hurry." She rounded ashes off her cigarette. "He's overall pretty sound. One of the better ones. He had a heart attack before he came here. Now mostly it's a bit of this, a bit of that. At eighty-two it adds up. Arthritis, hypertension, some senility. I know, it's a term that's gone out of favor, but it's descriptive. His electrical contacts aren't always sharp, so he gets a fair amount of channel noise at times, but he can be real lucid too. And persnickety. He'll probably tell you we're dosing his food with saltpeter, and that the nurses' reports of pinched butts is wishful thinking." Her laugh was both amazement and exasperation.

Perhaps aware that she'd been unloading, Nurse Wackowski took a last whispery drag of the cigarette and stubbed it out. "On good days, I'm dynamite." She matched Frank's smile with one of her own. "Come on, he should be done now."

The dayroom was white and airy, and the sunlight spilling across durable sage green carpet flecked with rose gave the impression of being cool. Close to twenty people sat in comfortable high-backed chairs, some watching a big TV with a noisy cartoon show in progress, others playing board games with staff members. A few gazed into space, slack-jawed and vacant, tuned to some private channel. The room might have been a preschool classroom, except for the smells: the air had the unmistakable tang of medicine and old age. Barb Wackowski led Frank over to a grizzled, wiry little man who sat apart, looking out a window. His sparse hair was pasted flat across his small, freckled head.

"Mr. Merloni? You have a visitor."

The old man gave no reaction. A gaunt woman in a bathrobe and pink slippers seemed interested though. She had shuffled over to stare at Frank. Gently, Barb Wackowski sent her back to the others.

"This is Mr. Branco," the nurse went on. "He knows your niece, Jane."

Lou Lou Merloni was in khaki slacks and an off-white shirt with large wing collars. His shave had left patches of whiskers and razor nicks on the wattle under his chin. Frank wondered if he had a hearing aid turned off.

"Mr. Merloni, I'm Frank Branco. I understand you like baseball." He sent a glance at the nurse. "And that you used to be called Lou Lou."

The old man turned now, his eyes murky and only vaguely aware. Barb Wackowski said, "Why don't the two of you visit," and with a reassuring pat on the old man's bony shoulder and a nod at Frank, she went off.

Frank drew over a chair and sat. It was warm there beside the window, the outside tropical heat sapping the cool inside air. "I was hoping we could talk baseball," Frank said.

The old man kept his silence a moment longer, then he said, "I know why they clean it." His voice was a smoky rasp.

"I'm sorry?"

"Nobody here uses it. Hell, we'd all drown. But I know why they keep it clean."

The pool. He was referring to the swimming pool. Beyond the window and a wire fence, a man with a long pole was skimming a turquoise rectangle of water.

"Why?" Frank asked.

"Account of the angels at night."

"The angels?"

"I've seen 'em. When no one's looking. They take off their wings and in they go, naked as the day God made 'em."

Frank drew a slow breath, thinking of airfare, car rental, the motel room, the time it had cost to get here. Patiently he opened the brown envelope and slid out the picture Jason Frawley had loaned him. He held it up for Lou Lou to see. The old man looked at it a moment, then looked away, remote. Frank set the photo down. He wiped perspiration from his face. There was a 3:30 flight to Boston. He could make it.

"Nineteen fifty-seven," Lou Lou Merloni said, still looking outside. "That's the Polo Grounds. If I had two cents for every sack of goobers I peddled in that joint, hey I'd be sitting pretty now." He turned to face Frank.

Frank slid his chair closer. "Do you remember those days?"

"Course I do."

"And you know who these players with you are?"

"That's Danny O'Connell, Jack Livingstone, and Herb Frawley. Okay?" His eyes glared.

"Okay. I'm interested in Herb Frawley. Did you know he died recently?"

"Herb died?" It seemed to confound him. He fingered his freckled forehead. "I thought that was O'Connell. He died too. How old was Herb?"

"Not yet sixty."

"I'm sorry to hear that. He was a nice fellow, Herbie. He died, huh?"

"In a car crash."

Merloni was silent another moment. "We were the Three Musketeers, Herb and Jack and me. We'd pal around Broadway, go to restaurants, nightclubs." The old eyes considered Frank, a little softer than they had been, beginning to be engaged. "A friend of Jane's you say?"

"I've met her. I'm a private investigator from Boston. Herb Frawley's former wife hired me to look into his death."

"Why do you want me?"

Frank explained the link from Bill Rigney to Floyd Tillman to the old card sharp at Coney Island. "I looked up your niece at Ocean Grove."

"Tinker to Evers to Chance." Lou Lou chewed his lip a moment, then leaned forward and tapped Frank's knee. "Everyone always said that, didn't they. Tinkers to Evers to Chance. Damn

Cubbies. Always overrated, you ask me. Cubbies this, Cubbies that! Who the hell does Harry Carey think he is?"

"I wanted to ask you about—"

"Reese to Herman to Camilli. Now that was a double-play combo." Merloni drew back, hands raised in preemptive surrender. "I know, I know. I'm not supposed to like the crosstown rivals, but god*damn*, they could throw the leather around. You always heard about Pee Wee, the little bastard. Even Billy Herman. But the real athlete in that combo was Dolf Camilli. He only played five, six years with the Dodgers, but boy was he good. Lifetime two-seventy-something hitter, a ton of home runs. It was a sad day in Brooklyn when he left."

He paused, pondering old sorrows, perhaps; then he squinted an eye at Frank. "Boston, huh?" He cackled. "That town always thought they could give the Yanks a run for the money. Good luck. Hey, they ain't done it yet, they ain't going to. Am I right?"

"I don't know," Frank said. "Nothing's forever."

"Damn bean-eaters! Still, those Boston teams have turned out some great players. Speaking of double-play combos, Boston had one of the best ever. Cronin to Doerr to Foxx. That's Jimmie, not Nellie." His face scrunched up in a wink. "See, kid, this old peanut pusher still knows his players. Uh . . ."

Merloni faltered, his grin sagged. "Why you here again?"

Frank told him, but almost at once the old man's mind had strayed off again, telling tales excerpted from the decades of his life in baseball. At times he spoke with a clarity of recall that gave Frank hope—citing games, individual performances, dates—but then, without warning, his memory grew random and disconnected. He gave fuzzy accounts wherein players of one generation stood alongside others who had yet to be born when the first group had already been long retired. Twice he interrupted himself to ask if Frank had any cigars. From time to time Frank would nudge him back from some rambling digression with mention of Herb Frawley. A nurse's aide brought medication and held the cup while Merloni drank through a flex straw, some of the liquid zigzagging down his chin in a pink trail.

Hot, frustrated, Frank brought up Herb Frawley one last time—and something strange happened. Lou Lou Merloni blinked, as if up to now the name had not fully penetrated some fog. "Herb Frawley," he murmured. "Boy, he coulda been a great one. I always said that. Y'ever see him play?"

"No," Frank said.

"Made the longest run for a catch I ever seen. He was playing center field one night his rookie year. Mays, who normally played center, was out with a gimp knee or somethin'. Now Frawley to that point had been in right field, and doing a good job. But this one night, he's in center, and they're playing . . ." He scratched at his high, freckled brow. "The Pirates. I know that on account of what I'm gonna tell you. Ralph Kiner comes up to the plate. Just a youngster himself, Kiner, and after taking a couple pitches, he drives—and I mean *drives*—a fastball on a clothesline to center. You ever see a game at the Grounds?"

"No," Frank said.

Merloni gave a cackling laugh. "Center field was this deep narrow corridor some wiseacre sportswriter dubbed Dead Man's Valley. Almost impossible to field a ball on the fly in that part of the park. What the fielders would do is chase it down on the roll, or just say the hell with it and concede an inside-the-park homer." He cackled again, paused, then blinked. "Uh, what was I talking about?"

"Ralph Kiner hitting a drive," Frank said.

"A drive."

"Toward Herb Frawley."

"Hell, yeah. So Kiner put everything he had into that one. The ball come off his bat like a rocket on the Fourth of July, and it's heading straight for Dead Man's Valley. Kiner breaks into a trot thinking he's got at least a triple out of the deal, and so is everyone else. I mean it was a shot! But that kid Frawley, he's deep out in the Valley now, having lit out soon as he heard the crack of the bat. And he's running, lean and quick. Well, son of a bitch if he doesn't put up his glove. Like the Statue of Liberty, see, and in goes the ball. He musta run fifty yards for it and he got it! Kiner's just rounding third and turns to see the Giants running off the field. And bringing up the rear, with the biggest pie-eating grin you ever seen, is Herb Frawley."

Lou Lou Merloni shook his head admiringly, as if seeing it all again on replay. "Say what you want about Herb—and there were fans and writers said some pretty savage things at the end there— but he was one of the best defensive players I ever seen. As good as Willie Mays. And his arm. Oh, what an arm! Like a cannon. I used to see him during pregame take a ball and peg it in from the deepest part of the outfield to home plate on one bounce. That's about five hundred feet, son. He and Mays used to have contests to see who could throw the farthest. Frawley won his share, I'll tell you.

"The boy could hit too. Not a power hitter, but just a good pure hitter who could spray the ball all over like a horny skunk. Don't get me wrong, he could jack it out of the park on occasion, but he wasn't going to give you forty dingers a year—unless he'd played up there in Fenway." Merloni cackled again. "But he could give you twenty in a season, and a hunert percent hustle. His offensive game reminds me a lot of that kid from Milwaukee, Molitor. Then, just as fast, he turned into Bob Lennon."

"Who?"

"A stiff, that's who. A first-class stiff." Merloni sighed, some of his energy seeming to escape with the breath. He sagged a little and shook his head. "If only his game hadn't gone to ruin the way it did. Nineteen fifty-seven it started."

"His slump," Frank said.

"Slump, schlump. I never bought that hula-hula. It was more than that. His game went down like a dive-bomber. Y'ever see him play?"

"No."

"Something got to him, caused him to . . . I don't know—quit."

Frank bent nearer, feeling himself close to the fragile edge of a discovery. "What did it?" he asked softly.

The old eyes seemed to flare more brightly for a moment. "I think it happened right here in Sarasota, in spring training." Merloni opened his mouth as if to speak, then shut it. Slowly his jaw sagged, the glow in his eyes fading. He shut them and leaned back in the chair. "I'm awful tired," he sighed.

"What were you about to say?" Frank pressed. "Can you remember anything specific? Anything that might've happened to cause those problems with his game?"

But the little man had fallen asleep.

At the desk in the nurses station, Barb Wackowski looked up. "How'd it go?"

"He's a talker when he gets going."

"A lot of them are if they find a patient listener—which you must be. You were in there two hours."

"He's napping now."

She nodded. "The short-term memory gets shaky—ask them about yesterday and you're liable to hear about last Christmas. But the long-term stuff can be sharp as a razor. Of course, it can drop off in a blink."

"Would it be okay if I came back later?"

"Today? Sure, why not? Visiting hours till seven."

At the door, Frank paused and went back. "Is he . . . I don't know the proper term for it—delusional?"

He recounted Lou Lou Merloni's story about angels in the swimming pool. By the time he finished, Nurse Wackowski's pale brown skin had taken on a becoming flush. "That sly old thing. That was this past Fourth of July. I had graveyard shift, but some of the nursing staff wanted to celebrate somehow. So after medications and lights-out, a few of us went in the pool." She shook her head and smiled. "Skinny-dipping. He must've spied."

15

FRANK WENT BACK TO THE MOTEL, THINKING TO TAKE A swim. The heat, and trying to follow the thread of the old man's rambling, had sapped him. In his room, the red message light on the phone was blinking. The desk told him Gilchrist had telephoned. He returned the call. Gilchrist said he had talked to a contact and learned a few added details on Herb Frawley's days in the Mexican baseball league, where he had played center field for the Mexico City Tigers.

"He got the job through some connections and went down in late spring of sixty-two. He got set up living with a friend of a friend outside the city. Apparently he played okay ball, but if it was a genuine comeback, we'll never know."

"Why not?"

"It didn't last. *He* didn't. Nobody's sure why. Midway through the season, he just booked. Left everything behind, not a word to anyone. Left with the clothes on his back. Wound up in a Mexican hospital awhile with the d.t.'s, then flew back to L.A. That was it for Herb Frawley and baseball."

Frank said he would be flying home himself the next day. He

recounted his meeting with Lou Lou Merloni and signed off. He lazed in the swimming pool awhile, had lunch, and at 3:30 he went back to Eventide Senior Care Center. It wasn't clear that Merloni remembered him right away, but again, by showing him the old photograph, Frank got him talking. He nudged the conversation around to Herb Frawley's last season in the majors.

"Yeah, it was a sad end," Merloni said. "He told me he thought about storming into Bob Scheffing's office—he was the manager at the time—and rearranging the furniture. But instead, he just got this feeling of . . . finality. He emptied his locker, packed up, then headed for the closest bar—only, as he pulled out of the parking lot, he changed his mind and headed south. For here."

"Sarasota?"

Merloni nodded. "Showed up at Alligator Al's. The Giants were gone by then, of course. Training in Phoenix, so the faces were changed. But old Alligator Al Elliott was still pouring the drinks. I happened to be in there that night, having dinner with my sister, Jane's mother. Hey, I was the one told Herb he oughta give Mexico a try. In fact, I arranged for him to stay with a guy I knew down there. But none of that really worked out. What was he there, a coupla months?"

"Any idea why he quit?"

Merloni shook his head. "I never seen him again after that night in Alligator Al's."

"Did you ever have any sense as to why he went downhill so quickly?"

"In the show?" Again the old man shook his head. "But sometimes I used to have this feeling . . . if he just coulda gone back to that first, shining season. All of us—Herbie, Jack, me—maybe things coulda been different."

"Different how?"

Something like pain twisted the old man's face—at not expressing it clearly, perhaps, or not being able to. Then it was gone and he looked away. After a silence, he said, "Cherchez la femme."

Frank glanced outside, expecting to see a nurse using the

swimming pool, but there was no one. The water lay flat and bright as cobalt glass.

"There was a woman," Merloni said in a soft rasp, still gazing toward the pool.

"One of the angels?"

"Long time ago. With Herb and Jack. She was a pretty thing. Dark curly hair . . . young. Always around."

"Around the ballpark?"

"Sure. Used to come for BP. Hang around afterward, too."

Frank tried to think if Nola Frawley had had dark hair in those days. He didn't think so. "One of the wives?" he asked. "Or girl-friends?"

Merloni rocked his head impatiently. "No, no."

"What are we talking about?" Frank asked. "Who is she?"

"Find that young woman. Ask her."

"Ask her what?"

The old man's face crinkled in a leathery maze of lines. "Everything."

Frank waited until seven o'clock to call, and as he picked up the phone to punch out the number on the Cape, he realized he was nervous. He had been thinking about Nola all afternoon. She wasn't at the gallery. Zoe told him Mrs. Dymmoch might be at home. She wasn't. He left a message that he would try again later. He went out and had supper at a seafood place on Gulf Drive and called again when he got back at 8:30. Nola sounded glad to hear from him. They traded small talk for a moment, then he said, "I want to ask you something. It might be painful."

"Frank, what is it?"

"It's about Herb. I need a candid answer."

"Please ask."

"You told me that the . . . energy in your marriage dwindled."

"It's true."

"Did he have other women?"

"Herb? Running around?"

"I know this is awkward."

Her response was a soft laugh. "You're a tender man for a tough investigator, Frank Branco. The answer is no."

"There was no one?"

"No women, no girlfriend. And don't feel awkward. I hired you to do your job. Don't let our . . . friendship get in the way, Frank. He simply wasn't the type who fooled around. His only mistress was baseball."

Frank felt a weight gone from him. "Okay, thanks. For the lecture too."

"I mean it. You can be totally candid with me."

He told her about his visits with Lou Lou Merloni. "He remembers some things vividly, but it's all jumbled together and hard to follow. I just wanted to gauge how much I can credit."

"What did he say?"

"He said I should talk to a woman, but he knew nothing about her. Dark haired and pretty, he said."

"He linked her to Herb?"

"No, not really. He was vague."

"I can't help with that. Sorry. Did he offer anything else?"

"He mostly said that the good old days were good old days. That Herb could have been one of the greats."

There was a soft, plaintive note in Nola's laugh. "That part is certainly true."

The conversation drifted back to incidentals, to art and Florida heat and what each had had for supper. As Frank got ready to say good-bye, he remembered something else. "Do you know anything about Herb's comeback try in Mexico?"

"It didn't work out, I know that. But we'd lost all contact by that point."

Everyone had, apparently. "Well, I think I'm going to fly back in the morning."

"Is that the end of it, then?"

"There might be some more things to do." Frank mentioned

his conversation with Gilchrist and said that Gilchrist was going to look into what players were in Cooperstown the weekend Frawley died, but Frank didn't expect much. They talked another minute, but there was no more light shed on old mysteries.

Nola said, "There's a lovely moon over the water. Can you see it from where you are?"

"I'm in a hermit's cave—a nice cold one."

When he had hung up, he parted the curtain. A slim moon was rising over the Vacancy sign. The telephone startled him. A woman said, "Mr. Branco?"

It was Jane Syrk. She had gotten his location from the nursing supervisor at Eventide. "I talked with my uncle on the phone. What did you say to him? He was *very* disturbed after your visit. He didn't know me at first."

"I'm sorry. I didn't mean to upset him."

"I'm the only family Uncle Lou has in this world. He's not in the best of health, and I have a real burden for his soul. I think you know that."

"I'm sorry, Jane. I didn't go there to bother him. I was hoping he'd remember things. I'm not going again."

"The visit *did* upset him. From the way he sounded, I'd say he's in some kind of crisis. I don't know what you talked about. It isn't important. What *is* is his soul. What I'm asking . . . what I'd like you to do—would you go back to see him again?"

Frank was confused. "I thought you said—"

"I'm trusting the Lord on this, Frank. Will you go back tomorrow and speak with my uncle one more time?"

16

Lou Lou Merloni was sitting alone by the window, oblivious to the too-loud television game show or the jigsaw puzzles and board games which gripped the attention of most of his fellow patients. He blinked in momentary absence as Frank settled into a vinyl chair across from him, then grinned. "Hey, Jane said you'd be back. Good to see you."

"I brought you these." Frank laid issues of *Baseball Weekly* and *The Sporting News* on the low ledge that ran along the window. Merloni acknowledged them with a glance, then leaned forward in his chair and tapped Frank's knee. "Hey, how'd you come acrost me again?"

Frank replayed the story: New York, Coney Island, Ocean Grove. "You make an impression on people."

"You ever meet a peanut man from the Polo Grounds before?"

"Never."

"Ain't many still around." Merloni sat back and preened.

"Yesterday we were talking about Herb Frawley," Frank said. "You told me I should talk to a young woman. Who is she?"

"I said that?"

"Yes. Dark-haired and pretty, you said."

Merloni's small face scrunched in a cartoon of concentration. Yesterday's patches of whiskers had been shaved, replaced by new ones. "Maybe I was talking ragtime," he rasped. "All this medicine they give me. A woman, jeez, I don't know." His eyes brightened. "Hey, I ever tell you about the time Johnny Mize whacked one into the right-field seats where I'm working? Ball landed smack in my basket, sent red hots flying every which way. Afterward I got Mize to sign it."

Another patient wheeled over, whom Frank recognized as the ancient soldier in the VFW cap. The man watched until Lou Lou gave him *The Sporting News* and sent him away. As he had yesterday, Merloni began to talk, growing animated with the zest of remembering. Today he was recalling his youth. He had grown up in the Hell's Kitchen section of New York, quit school young. But he didn't go on the con like some of his friends did. "Uh-uh. I could've. I knew the street good as I knew my own back pocket. But, I was brung up right, know what I mean?" He gave his canny, self-parodying grin. "Nah, I wasn't gonna rip no one off. Eventually I got the ballpark job, and I liked it. Where's the future pushing park food, friends would say, but this was the depression remember, and I was happy to work and watch the ball games. I stuck with it."

Never having married or had a family, the Giants took on that role, and Merloni built a life around baseball. "Winters I'd come down here when the team had training. What that did, it gave me a chance to know the players personal. There was always free time, so we'd hang out, play cards, whatnot. Have some laughs. I was never one for golf, but fishing though . . . There was good fishing all over Florida in them days. I went with Ted Williams one time when he came east from Scottsdale. Bonefishing over in the Keys. Best hitter the game's ever known, Williams. Hell of a fisherman too. Over here, some of the guys liked to go out deep-sea, on a boat. Not me. Made me seasick, you want to know the truth. Freshwater's my idea of fishing. We'd fish the Myakka River, and the Little Manatee. There was this one place I used to take some of the guys. A little sinkhole pond. You know, after workouts, bring some cerveza and some Cubano cigars." He waggled fingers in a Groucho Marx gesture. "Jeez, I ain't thought of this stuff in years. I'm glad you came. Uh ..." He ran a hand over his patchy cheek. "What was your name again?"

Lou Lou Merloni went on, peeling layers, pausing as he lost a thought, picking up another and working with it until that too strayed. Little of what he said bore relevance to Frank's questions, but Frank was patient; this would be his last try with the old man. He waited for little openings to lead the monologue back to Herb Frawley. Time passed, marked by the coming and going of staff members with lunch, medications, the changing programs on the dayroom TV.

"On account of I was older than the players, and I'd grown up in the city, I knew the streets," Lou Lou said. "I took to being a rabbi."

"A rabbi?" Frank said.

"Uh . . . a fixer, you know. Guys wanted a bottle of good champagne, box of Monte Cristos—B.F. this woulda been: before Fidel—when you could still get the good ones. I'd get the guys whatever they wanted. Reefer? Okay, sure. Never used it myself, but if a guy wanted it . . . I mean, what the hell, it didn't hurt his talent. Hey, they wanted to crucify Robert Mitchum. For what? A coupla lousy sticks a pot. Now there was an actor for you, Mitchum. You remember that picture with Marilyn Monroe? *River of No Return?*"

"What else did you do for the players?" Frank asked.

Merloni's eyes crinkled with silent laughter. "Yeah, okay, I'll tell you. Somebody wanted to lay off a little dough on a horse race, golf game? I'd take the action. I'd bring it to people I knew who'd cover it. You think Rose is the first player to gamble? He was just cocky about it." He sighed. "Then, of course, some of the guys dug ladies."

"Tell me about that," Frank said.

"These'd be girls I knew who liked to be around ballplayers. Party stuff, after hours."

"In New York?"

"New York *and* here. Mostly here. They were all over Florida when the ball teams were around. Camp followers. Not hookers, I'm talking. No money changed hands—or not much. They just dug the kicks."

"When you said, 'Find the woman,' did you mean one of those?"

Merloni scratched at his sparse hair and frowned. "I don't know what I meant." He shrugged. "Anyways . . ."

Each recollection seemed to spring other long-forgotten memories, which the old man told with the relish of a reformed sinner: drug dealer, numbers runner, pimp—fixer for boy-men with money in their pockets and time on their hands—in his own mind, as vital to the ball club as the coaches and manager. Frank let him talk, wondering though if this was the sort of confession that Jane Syrk would consider good for the soul. When a nurse had dispensed afternoon medications, Frank produced the old photograph again and nudged the conversation back to spring training of 1957.

Lou Lou Merloni squinted at the photograph once more, then turned to look out the window to where a middle-aged couple in cabana wear were negotiating an ancient woman toward the parking lot. It was a slow process, but finally they got her into a silver-gray Cadillac and drove off. Still gazing out, Merloni said, "He was a regular hoochie-coochie man. Girls in every town they played. But girlfriends he wasn't interested in."

"Frawley had a lot of women?"

"Damn it, you listening?" Merloni swung around. "Livingstone I'm talking. His old man was a meatpacker, nasty son of a bitch. Probably where Jack got his mean streak. That happens with people, it keeps running downhill. Jack, he used to be kinda . . ."

Merloni blew his breath out hard. His high forehead had begun to perspire, and he was fidgeting in the chair like he needed a bathroom.

"Are you all right?"

"Yeah."

"Go on," Frank urged.

"The weird stuff."

"What do you mean?"

"Kinks, you know? C'mon, help me here."

"Kinky sex?"

"Handcuffs, mouth gags, like that."

"You got those things for Jack Livingstone?"

"Nah, he musta got 'em himself."

"So where did you come in?"

Merloni turned toward the window again, clearly agitated. Frank wondered if they should continue. Frank glanced across the dayroom, looking to see if one of the nurses was nearby. None was, but a candy striper was feeding an old woman in pink sponge-rollers. If need be, she could summon a nurse.

"What did you fix for Jack Livingstone, Lou? Women?"

Merloni rubbed his throat, the whiskers ticking against his palm. He swung the hand outward. "Movies, mostly, y'know?"

"Movies. Porno films?"

"You couldn't get 'em just anywheres in them days, not like now. A guy I knew on Forty-second Street—he could get 'em. Used to make 'em. Hey, what can I tell you, all right? You asked. Movies and books. Jack was a little weird."

"Did Herb Frawley get involved with that?" Frank was thinking of the unopened videocassette in Frawley's apartment in Utica.

Merloni's face crumpled. His mouth seemed to chew in on itself, like the outward manifestation of his memory, and he rubbed at it with brown-blotched hands. Across the dayroom the old woman in sponge-rollers had gotten into an escalating argument with a soap opera actress, apparently blaming the woman for betraying her with someone named Dr. Samson. The candy striper was attempting to distract her with a bowl of Jell-O. Frank tried to shut them out, wanting to probe the vein Merloni's restless memory had uncovered.

"Was Herb Frawley involved in that?"

"Sometimes . . . people get into things they don't mean to. . . . They—" He broke off, a dazed look sweeping his face.

"Was Frawley involved?"

Merloni shook his head. "No. He was a good kid, Herb. Quiet and respectful. I told ya."

"Would there have been any reason for Herb Frawley to try to blackmail anyone?"

"Huh? What're you talking about? That don't sound like Herb. Blackmail. You mean *now?* Why don't you go ask him?"

The conversation went on a while longer, but it led nowhere, and Frank realized he had learned all he was going to. It was time to go back to Boston, check in with Gilchrist, present what little he knew to Nola, perhaps give Jane Syrk a call and tell her he had come. As he stood up and began to thank Lou Lou Merloni, the old man suddenly clutched Frank's wrist.

Frank waited. The brown-speckled hand was surprisingly tight on his wrist. "What is it?"

"Let me show you," Lou Lou Merloni said.

"Show me what?"

The sharp old eyes met Frank's with an aggrieved stare, then shifted away. "What you came for," Merloni whispered.

The Garcia y Vega filled the car with its aroma. Frank kept his window cracked just enough to draw the smoke out. He had had to clear the outing with Barb Wackowski when she came on duty, but it wasn't a big deal. Patients took family visits all the time. She had given Frank a list of instructions and had him sign a release form. Cigars were not on the list, though they weren't forbidden either, as Merloni himself made clear. The old man had dressed himself, up to and including the big wraparound sunglasses. Sitting there in a straw fedora his niece had given him, and an old but well-kept Palm Beach jacket, he was as excited as a kid on a school field trip.

They had stopped twice: at the smoke shop, and once again at a tourist information booth for a map and directions. Now Frank drew up to the corner of Twelfth Street and Tuttle Avenue.

"Is that it?"

They looked over at Ed White Stadium, since 1960 the spring-training home of the Chicago White Sox. Before that, the Giants had played there. But clearly changes had taken place, and this fact seemed to agitate the old man, as though a once stable surface had been yanked out from under him, upsetting some ancient compass. He squirmed in his seat and stared out at the stadium, the big dark glasses giving him an insectlike intentness. "Lemme see that map again," he said with something like panic in his voice.

Afternoon heat wrinkled the air so that the red and black words shimmered against the white particleboard background.

CASTLE HILL ESTATES
OFFERED BY PALMETTO REALTY
3- AND 4-BEDROOM UNITS, $49,900 AND UP
ATTRACTIVE TERMS

Some kind of pink-flowering vine was in the process of over-running the sign, and gun toters had blasted holes in it. Alongside it, at a right angle to the empty two-lane east-west state road where they were stopped, lay a narrow entry road. They were a dozen miles east of Sarasota, in an area of citrus groves. Frank looked at Lou Lou Merloni. "Well?"

The old man gummed the cigar a long moment, then nodded.

The paved entry road quickly gave way to dirt, rutted by the passage of heavy vehicles and baked to hardpan. They passed several dusty trailer homes set back among clumps of palmetto. Otherwise the land was groves. Farther on they came to a branching road, marked by a set of stucco pillars. There might once have been a chain or a gate between them, but there was nothing now. Merloni frowned, uncertain again, then gestured for Frank to go through. A short way in sat a house under construction. This apparently was to be a model for Castle Hill Estates, though there were no castles around, or hills for that matter. The particleboard had faded to gray and sheets of foil wrap hung loose. The lot was being reclaimed by saplings.

Frank stopped, convinced that Lou Lou Merloni was lost, navigating aimlessly by a decades-old mental map. After Ed White Stadium, they had driven around Sarasota looking for a restaurant and bar Lou Lou claimed was a favorite drinking hole for him and some of the Giants players, including Jack Livingstone and Herb Frawley. Alligator Al's it had been called, the place where years later, Merloni remembered, he had met a washed-up and drunk Frawley. They found no trace of it.

"What are you stopping for?" Lou Lou said irritably. "It's in here."

Frank sighed. "What is? What are we supposed to be looking for?"

"I'll tell you when we get there. Keep going—it can't be much farther."

It wasn't. Ahead the road curved and went down a slight decline, and there beyond a tangle of trees, water glinted in sunlight. Lou Lou Merloni thumped the dashboard. "I was right! That's it!"

"You're sure?"

"This is where I'd come fishing with Jack and Herb." He was already fumbling with his seat-belt latch.

Frank drove nearer and parked. He helped the old man out. The banks of the little pond were thickly overgrown. Frank assisted Merloni, who used an aluminum cane with small rubber-capped feet at the bottom. It was slow going, but he insisted that they get right to the edge of the pond. "Damn the mosquitoes," he said. Frank forged a trail through the bushes, and they emerged finally in a small, dusty clearing.

Breathing hard from the exertion, Lou Lou stood gazing at the water. Half the pond was covered with lily pads, among the flowers of which blue dragonflies darted. With the scum of weeds and the reflection of the sky, it was hard to tell how deep the water was, but if it was a sinkhole, as Merloni had said, it could be very deep. Lou Lou had fallen silent, staring at the pond. Thinking of what? Fish he had once caught here? Cerveza and Cuban cigars? Skinny-dipping angels?

A minute went by. Except for the drone of insects and birds, the place lay stunned in the afternoon heat. Drawn by the prospect of new blood, mosquitoes were mounting an attack, but they moved sluggishly and were easy to kill. Frank wiped his brow. "What did you want to show me?" he said.

The old man said nothing.

"Maybe we should get back."

Merloni shuffled a few steps sideways, stirring dust. He shifted his grip on the cane, and lifted a hand, as if to swat a mosquito, but Frank saw he was pointing at something, or trying to. His hand trembled. Frank looked to see what he was pointing at, but sunlight was flaring on the surface of the water.

"What is it?" he asked.

The old man started to sway.

"Are you all right?" Frank said, suddenly nervous.

Merloni stumbled forward, and his hat fell off. He would have fallen into the water if Frank hadn't grabbed him. Frank got him back to the car, into the seat. Merloni's breathing was quick and shallow, his face flushed with exertion. Was he having a heart attack? Frank took off the sunglasses.

"Do you have any pain?"

"I'm okay," Lou Lou rasped. But his eyes looked frightened.

"I'm taking you home."

"Yeah . . . better do that." As he got the car turned around, Frank looked at Merloni. He had his eyes shut and was whispering fiercely. It sounded like a string of curses. Frank had to concentrate on the narrow, rutted road, driving as fast as he dared. Dust stormed behind the car. He reached over and put a reassuring hand on the old man's arm, but Lou Lou continued to whisper. Only after they had reached the state road and Frank picked up speed did he remember he had forgotten to retrieve the straw hat. That's also when he realized that Lou Lou Merloni wasn't cursing at all.

No, he was praying.

17

IT WAS GOING ON 5:30 WHEN FRANK FOUND THE DIRT ROAD again, and passed through the pillared entrance of Castle Hill Estates, past the fading, unfinished model home. The sunlight was coppery in the trees encircling the sinkhole pond. Dust still hung in the air as though from his passage not two hours ago. He hiked in to the spot where Lou Lou Merloni had stood. The old man had murmured prayers all the way back to Eventide Senior Care Center. There, his face gray with fatigue, he had been taken by wheelchair to an examining room, and from there to his bed. Frank waited until Nurse Wackowski reappeared, her pale brown features compassionate.

"He's resting," she said. "His pulse and blood pressure are okay, but we'll monitor him. We've got him on a glucose IV and medication. What happened?"

Frank told her.

"And it just came on suddenly?"

"I thought he was pointing at something, and next thing he started to keel over. I hope it wasn't the cigar."

She shook her head. "It's the heat, and probably the exertion."

"I lost his hat."

"He can get another. I think he'll be all right."

"I hope so. I'm sorry."

"No one's fault. Like I said yesterday, living catches up on all of us."

He smiled. He'd bet she was one terrific nurse. He asked if he could see Lou Lou.

She went to consult the doctor, who said it would be okay, though only for a few minutes. Merloni had had enough excitement for one day; they wanted him to rest. Frank went into the room where the old man lay in semidarkness, with scarcely more color than the sheets. He seemed tethered to the bed with wires and tubes, and appeared to be sleeping. But as Frank stood there, Lou Lou opened his eyes. For an instant fear seemed to widen them, then recognition, and something else. Pleading? Merloni said something in a dry whisper. *Get out of here?* No; something else. Frank leaned closer, aware as he did that the smell of cigar had been displaced by the tart aromas of medicine and antiseptic. Over the thin beeping of a bedside monitor, the old man said, "Forget everything."

Frank found the straw fedora where Merloni had dropped it. He picked it up and looked out over the pond, hazy in the torpor of late afternoon. Birds and insects, silenced by his arrival, lifted their voices again. What had caused the old man's reaction? Was it the heat and exertion? Or something else? Frank stepped nearer to the water, looking down the weedy bank toward the spot where Lou Lou appeared to have been pointing.

On the surface a fish stirred, sending ripples away in concentric rings, like a target. Frank took off his shoes and socks and stripped off his pants. He went down the bank to the water and waded out. For a half dozen steps the muddy bottom angled gently underfoot, the tepid water deepening around his thighs. From its first touch, his mind had gone to the night with Nola Dymmoch in the ocean. He took another step and nearly fell.

The bottom was gone.

He bent close to the surface, peering past the shade of his cupped hands. The slope appeared to drop off sharply. The pond hardly seemed large enough to be deep; but obviously it was.

Debating for a moment, he emptied his lungs, drew them full, and eased below the surface. He swam down using his arms and legs, pressure building on his ears. After a few strokes, in blurred focus he could see the dark hole. The bottom lay far below. Too far. He turned back to the surface.

He climbed out and stood dripping on the bank, more fully aware now of his curiosity. It was probable, as Nurse Wackowski suggested, that Lou Lou Merloni had simply experienced heat exhaustion. He was an old man, acclimated to the cool indoor world of the retirement home. Or perhaps he had been reliving a long-ago day of fishing and adventure and had grown overexcited. But was it possible too that after all these years, some ghost still dwelled here? That a faded secret lay on that deep bottom? Frank wanted to find out.

In Palmetto he picked up the coast road, driving past chain restaurants, auto repair garages, truck stops, video stores, guns-and-ammo shops—the hundred small businesses that served the area. At last he found a marina where, among the signs of marine supplies and outboard motors, he saw the distinctive red flag with white slash that he hoped he would find. Inside the dive shop he went through the procedures of showing his certification card, conducting the rental transaction, and finally doing his own personal inspection, so that it was after seven o'clock by the time he passed for the third time the weathering pillars of Castle Hill Estates. The sun was already angling low beyond the trees as he stepped into the pond in brand-new swim trunks. Sitting in the shallows he pulled on the rubber fins, spat in the latex mask, rinsed it, and cupped it to his face. As Frank opened the tank valve and adjusted the mouthpiece, a water snake slithered across the pond twenty feet from him, heading for the lily pads. With a shiver, Frank paddled out.

He didn't have to swim far. He could clearly see the drop-off this time, sudden and steep, the light filtering down to deep green. He descended slowly, swimming with minor effort, easy enough in the fins and weight belt. In spite of a slight algae bloom, the visibility was good, descent easy. He reached twenty feet. The water density was different from the salty Atlantic, which wanted to push you back up, the better to hold on to its secrets. In his days with the police department's underwater recovery unit, the work had mostly been in the cold murk of the harbor and its tidal rivers, dank, forbidding places where often you groped along by feel, in search of an abandoned weapon, sodden articles of clothing, or worse. At least, however, you had an inkling of what you were looking for.

The depth gauge showed thirty feet.

Far above, light poked among the lily pads and sank in rusty shafts. For a moment he thought of his night with Nola Dymmoch, wondered if she had ever been scuba diving. Then he let it go.

Thirty-five feet.

And there was the bottom. It was silted and spread with rocks, a few sunken logs angled across it, fish, the occasional decaying beer can. Nothing that didn't belong.

Disappointment. Then: relief. Forget everything, Merloni had said. Good advice. Cross off another line of investigation. Frank gave a last scan of the dim green world before heading for the surface—and something nudged itself into awareness. Over there. Lying alongside one of the logs was a big rock, protruding from the top of which was something in the shape of a U. He swam closer and, peering at it, saw that it wasn't a rock at all. The U was one side of a handle attached to a long satchel. His heartbeat quickened.

For a slow moment he just looked at it. Algae and sediment

had given the bag the color of the bottom. Then, carefully, he prodded the side. He gripped the handle and pulled. There was an instant's resistance, then the handle tore away on one side, its fastener rusted through. The other handle was in the same condition. Moving closer to the satchel, he found the zipper tab at one end. Like the handles, it too was broken. Working from one corner, he carefully tore the fabric away from the zipper. When he had it halfway done, too eager to take time for the rest, he pulled open the bag. A swirl of silt rose from inside, making him back up instinctively, but in that moment before the water grew too cloudy to see, he made out what might have been several waterlogged baseball bats, and an old pair of baseball shoes.

His heart drummed faster. In the world of the living, baseball had seen ten thousand games played, heroes had emerged, teams had moved, their names changed; new teams had been created, stadiums built for men who had not even been born yet, a sport no longer of kids, but of men, cold-eyed and wealthy before their time. But down here, the only link with that upper world had been the occasional beer can tossed in, a fishing lure drawn through the calm depths, and the light that had sifted down in twelve thousand cycles of the sun, a light that was dwindling now as day waned. As the sediment settled, Frank worked his arms under the waterlogged canvas and lifted. The bag came loose from the bottom with a slight tug that raised another cloud of mud. Gripping the bag to his chest, he swam to the surface.

The satchel gurgled softly as it drained on the bank of the pond. Forcing himself to be patient, drawing on the habits of his cop training, Frank carried the scuba tank, weight belt, and fins to the car and put them into the trunk. He drew on his shirt. With the coming of dusk, the mosquitoes had renewed their attack. Sounds had changed: different birds called now. He went back through the tangle of trees to the pond, where he pulled away the rest of the zipper and opened the waterlogged bag.

Inside, in a brown gelatinous mass, tiny glassy worms squiggled. Gingerly he put his hand in and drew out a baseball bat. He could see the familiar Hillerich & Bradsby Co. trademark branded into the sodden ash. Louisville Slugger. Next came a pair of corroded leather shoes with rusty cleats, a wet baseball, and several fist-sized stones. Then his hand encountered something long and hard, knobbed on one end. But it wasn't another bat. He drew it into the fading light and saw that it was a bone.

The first soft pulse of fear beat in him then, and he squatted there, feeling it. Aware of being alone, he glanced toward the thicket, beyond which the car was invisible. He reached into the satchel again. Another bone. And reached again. Another. Leg bones, he was pretty sure; though he wouldn't say from what. His growing revulsion overcome by growing determination, he put his hand in again. And this time, his heart convulsed, not from any real surprise at what his fingers touched, but from a fatal sense of fulfillment of what he had thought would be there and prayed wasn't. A surge of bile stung the back of his throat. He swallowed it back and lifted the item out. Staring back at him with empty eye sockets was a human skull.

18

HE COULD NOT SAY HOW MUCH TIME PASSED. THE CLEARING had grown dusky with mosquitoes and night. Frank stared at the open mouth of the satchel, trying to deal with a thought that had quietly been forming since he had first opened the bag—maybe even earlier, maybe back when he and Nola had made love on the beach.

Let it be.

Forget everything. Merloni's words.

Put the bag back in the pond and let the water close in over thirty years of silence, let the earthmovers come and make way for Castle Hill Estates, three- and four-bedrooms units, starting at $49,900. He could walk away right now, drive to the motel, pack, get out to the airport. He still had Nola, didn't he? She wouldn't press him for reasons. All at once he had a desperate desire to see her.

He wedged these thoughts from his mind and reached into the bag once more. There were other bones, smaller, like radii and ulnas, ribs, knuckles, and toes: slimy with their years of immersion. There were more rocks and, in the bottom, two loops of rusted steel, which he realized were handcuffs. He made a neat pile of everything on the ground, and when the satchel was empty, there on the rubberized inner fabric, he found some markings inked there, just visible in the fading light. A name.

J. Livingstone.

Thirty minutes later, having returned the dive gear, he wanted a drink. But he drove past several night-lit restaurants and bars, aware with a cool tingle of paranoia that he did not want the company of people. He was carrying a secret, and it would be there, marked on him for strangers to detect. He glanced in the rearview mirror. Had that car been back there too long?

He had taken the items he'd earlier removed from the bag— handcuffs, rocks, bones, skull, shoes—and put them back in. He had waded out, shivering then, unable to imagine he had ever found the water warm. When his feet found the drop-off, he lowered the bag into the pond and allowed it to fill with water. He swung it out slowly like a silent bell. Heavy from its years of immersion, the bag sighed indolently, gasped once, then rolled over and sank in a trail of bubbles. Using the face mask, he checked to be sure the bag hadn't snagged close to the surface. It hadn't. It was gone. The only thing he had kept was the baseball.

He settled for a fifth of Jack Daniel's at a bottle shop and drove back to the hotel. He scrubbed his hands twice with soap and hot water. He poured an inch of whiskey over ice cubes. When he had drunk it, he called the Eventide Senior Care Center. A woman with a soft Hispanic accent told him that Nurse Wackowski had gone off duty, that Mr. Merloni was sedated and asleep.

"Will I be able to speak with him in the morning?" Frank asked.

"No, I don't think so," the woman said, speaking as gently as if she were in the room with Lou Lou Merloni. "His niece has asked that no one be allowed to talk to him."

"She's here?"

"She telephoned."

"What did she say?"

"Only that he should not speak with anyone."

Frank poured another two fingers of Jack Daniel's. His face was filmed with perspiration, his shirt sticky on his torso. He sat in the dark with the bottle propped between his thighs, Gilchrist-style. He would need to get hold of Jane Syrk, insist that she let him speak with her uncle. Then what? He tried to think past this place, this moment. Get the police? Definitely. But not yet. Too many questions. Not until he had spoken with Lou Lou Merloni. He didn't want to cause any more trouble for the old man than he already had. Or for himself; with each passing moment that became more clear. Frank understood that he was at some kind of Mendoza line, hanging in by his fingernails, so tentative in his grasp of events that perspective was denied him. He needed to know more.

In the bathroom he splashed his face. He picked up the waterlogged baseball. He gripped it along the swollen stitching, thinking . . . baseball without a commissioner, Pete Rose banned from the game for life, Dwight Gooden and Daryl Strawberry on drug suspensions. Lockouts and walkouts and crippling strikes, scandals, traveling mistresses, salaries no one could afford, journalists who had gone sour, and fans who were turning their backs on the game. He had the dizzying sense that baseball was no more the American pastime than anything else was, that the country was no longer stitched with any common thread.

But he resisted the notion. Somewhere kids were playing on a grassy field, girls included, and parents were cheering, people were eating hot dogs and drinking soda and beer, yelling for the home team, it was summer, and—

There was a knock on the motel-room door.

Frank had a quick dazzle of panic. Recovering, he set the wet baseball by the sink. He checked himself in the mirror, brushed back his hair. He shut off the light and closed the bathroom door.

When he opened the outer door, two people stood on the concrete walkway, imprecise figures in the dim glow of the bug light.

"Yes?" Frank said.

One of the figures stepped forward, yellow light spilling off round eyeglasses, and reached toward Frank's face. Something in the man's hand flashed.

19

"MR. BRANCO?" THE MAN SAID. THE BRIGHTNESS, FRANK saw now, was a policeman's shield.

"Yes?"

"Frank L. Branco?"

"Yes."

"Name is Cruz. From the Sarasota County Sheriff's office. This is Patrolman Lee." He said it without any trace of irony, despite the fact that the officer was a young woman.

"Is something wrong?" Frank asked.

Officer Lee, who had an eager, no-nonsense demeanor, aimed a flashlight at the rental car parked there in front of the motel unit. Frank hadn't noticed until now how dusty it was. "Is this the vehicle you're driving, sir?" Lee asked.

"Yes . . . that's mine. Is anything wrong?" he asked again.

"I hope not," Cruz said quietly. "That's kind of what we'd like to find out. You armed, Mr. Branco?"

"I may be the only one in the state who isn't, Sheriff."

"Yeah, well, we've got some real peckerwoods in the state-house."

The man was short and neckless, with a broad, thin-lipped mouth and puffy eyes behind the round gold-frame glasses. He fanned at a moth which eluded his hand and fluttered into the room. Frank said, "You might as well come in."

Cruz looked at Patrol*wo*man Lee, then at Frank. "You inviting us in?"

He was being careful to avoid any claim of rights violation later. But Frank could see no reason for that to worry him. He was more mystified than afraid. Why were they here? "Come on."

Once inside, Officer Lee was the busier of the two: looking around the room, peering quickly into the bathroom. Frank had the feeling she would have liked to probe the closet with her flashlight, go through his suitcase, jot things in her notebook. Cruz's interest was directed mostly at Frank. In the better light, Frank could see that he was in his late fifties. Because of his short stature, he kept his head tipped back into fleshy shoulders and gazed upward through his round glasses. With his wide mouth, he had the look of an amiable, vaguely ineffectual bullfrog. He seemed better suited to a desk patrol, not out knocking on motel-room doors after dark.

"What's going on?" Frank asked, his puzzlement giving way to annoyance.

Cruz took a chair at the circular Formica-top table. "We had a report that that car out yonder made a trip to Palmetto this afternoon, two passengers inside. Later, the same car was back again, twice, only one person aboard. That you?"

"A report? From whom?"

"That you?" Cruz repeated.

"Probably. Out by Castle Hill Estates? Yeah, I was there."

"There's a neighbor lives out that way's got nothing better to do all day than look out the window and make a nuisance of himself. The third time he called, we sent a car out—mostly to get him off our back, though there have been *in*cidents out that way."

Officer Lee flipped pages of her notebook. "I got out there when you were coming back through the gate. Eight-forty-four, that would've been. You came back to Route 41, stopped at Gulf Marine Scuba and returned dive gear, then stopped for a bottle." She glanced at the fifth of Black Jack. "You came here at nine-twenty-five, where you've been registered since the night before last."

So Frank's sense of being followed hadn't been just paranoia. He hadn't identified the unmarked county car.

"Meantime," said Cruz, "we called in the license tag and got your name and home address from the auto-rental office."

"Is that normal curiosity?"

"It probably would've ended there. Three trips makes me curious, but you weren't breaking any laws. But like I say, there've been incidents out at the Castle Hill site."

"Incidents?" Frank drew out a chair and sat down.

"Vandalism, mostly. Somebody blew up a bulldozer a while back. What red-flagged you, though—and the reason for this friendly visit—August's an off time to be coming to Gulf Coast Florida, Mr. Branco. Even for a private eye."

Despite his annoyance, Frank was impressed. "You learned that from the phone call?"

"PIs are state-licensed up there in Mass. My sources can tell me that."

Frank decided it would be best not to get cute. There was that manner about Cruz of a bullfrog looking to snap up a fly. He said, "I'd offer you a drink, but I know you're on the clock."

"*She* is." Cruz looked at Officer Lee. "See if there's an extra glass."

Lee went into the bathroom, turned on the light. Frank said, "Is it *Sheriff* Cruz?"

"Used to be. See, there's this law says a person's gotta quit when they hit a certain age, or take a desk assignment. Just plain Cruz is fine."

Officer Lee brought the glass, and Frank put in ice and poured. He watered both drinks, thinking he needed to slow this down.

Cruz tasted his, then asked, "Who was riding shotgun your first ride out there?"

"A man named Merloni. It was a field trip from a nursing home where he lives. Then I dropped him off. I can give you the name and number of the place if you want to check."

"What's the big interest in Castle Hill?"

"Nothing really. He remembered the area from years ago, when it was just grove land. He used to fish in the pond."

Cruz nodded. "That was going to be prime U.S.-inspected easy living out there. It sure looked good in the artist's drawings, anyhow. Only the builder was one sleek, greedy son of a bitch. Nothing unusual in that. His problem was he was also dumb as a stump. He was an out-of-towner who sold the lots to out-of-towners, based on a prospectus and a line of bull. He took the money and never got around to building anything beyond half the model home before he got hog-tied in red tape. EPA regulations, mostly, including that pond. He blew his money on a losing law case and finally ducked behind chapter eleven. The local trades-men ate their losses the best they could. Some of the investors have tried to pursue it through the state AG's office, which means it might get resolved next century. Then, ten months ago, the de-veloper ended up in a car trunk in Miami. Shot. The betting is one buyer figured his own way to handle it. My guess is a guy from Pas-saic, New Jersey, in the trash-disposal business according to records." Cruz shrugged—hard to do with no neck. "That's how we read it, though there's nothing'll ever prove it, 'less someone gets religion and decides to confess." He narrowed one eye behind the round lenses. "Or does something stupid."

"Interesting story," Frank said. "But it's all brand-new to me, Sheriff."

" 'Cruz' is good. Maybe you're hired by someone to make mis-chief, some other investor who got burned, or some—" He looked at Officer Lee. "What do they call them? The crowd's been in-volved in the beach thing?"

"Conservationists," she said.

"That other word the paper keeps using."

"Eco freaks?"

He turned back. "Who figure that pond's been poisoned and the land's been raped. Hell, nothing new there. That's the story of Florida. *Greeniks*, that's the word I was thinking. And maybe someone figures blowing up a bulldozer makes a statement. Or maybe you're with one of those junk TV shows that like to pretend they're journalists. Or was it just a sentimental journey for your nursing-home friend?" Cruz clapped a hand over his wide mouth. "I'm getting talky. Must be the hootch." He looked at the glass in his hand, from which Frank had seen him take only one sip. "And why'm *I* talking anyway? *You're* right here. You tell us." He leaned forward, setting the glass on the table, and looked expectantly at Frank. "Why were you out there?"

The cop's old-boy routine was masterful. Officer Lee stood by with her notebook and pen. Frank knew there was no point in trying to be tricky; but he didn't want to reveal what he had found. Not yet. Not until he had talked to Lou Lou Merloni, and to Nola.

"I *am* working," he said, "but not for anyone connected with that development deal. Before you just told me about it, I didn't know a thing about that. I'm trying to get information about a former baseball player. The old man at the nursing home used to know him. I was trying to jog his memory."

"Baseball player? Who?"

"Herb Frawley."

The cops only looked blank.

"What's in the pond?" Cruz asked.

Frank knew they could check his story easily enough, but he didn't think they would. There was no cause to. Cops weren't paid to go around looking for things to do: budgets and time were in too short supply to worry about crimes that hadn't been committed; though Cruz seemed to have an uncommon disregard for both. Frank shook his head. "I haven't come up with anything that makes sense. If I do . . . if I discover that any of what I'm looking at involves something you should know, I will tell you."

Cruz nodded. "I'll expect it."

As the cops were leaving, Frank waited for Officer Lee to get outside before he said, "Cruz."

The man turned, yellow light spilling off the lenses of his glasses. Frank said, "Thirty years ago, was there any unsolved case involving the disappearance of a young woman?"

"Around here?"

Frank hesitated, glanced toward Lee climbing into the un-marked county car. "This might've been in the late winter or spring of nineteen fifty-seven."

"Maybe I should be asking *you?*"

"I don't know."

"Why the curiosity, Branco?"

"It's professional."

As Officer Lee put on the headlights, movement caught Frank's eye. Something scuttled across the parking area, into the bushes. Cruz read Frank's glance.

"Armadillo," he said. "They've made their way over from East Texas over the years. Dumb little suckers get out in the road, and the car lights freeze 'em. Maybe they think they're invulnerable on account of their shell, and a few million years of being around. Tell that to a steel-belt radial on a two-ton Caddy doing seventy. *Bango!* That's all she wrote." He turned back to Frank. "Professional, you said."

"I'll keep my word to you," Frank promised.

Cruz gave a slow nod and drew a card from the pocket of his faded khaki shirt. He handed it to Frank. "We'll see."

20

THE DREAM WAS BROKEN PIECES. NOLA JOGGING TOWARD him down the long golden curve of Race Point Beach. Her lips soft and cool on his. Scuttling armadillos. What had shattered the dream rang again. Frank reached for the phone.

"Had coffee yet?"

The voice was a rusty croak, and Frank spent an opaque few seconds before identifying it. It was the last voice he had heard last night. How long ago had that been? Eight hours? Ten? The motel-room drapes showed only a crack of daylight, in which the mostly empty Jack Daniel's bottle glinted. "What time is it?"

"Good, you haven't had morning coffee," Cruz said. "It's on me." Cruz gave an address. Frank repeated it, and the cop was gone.

Twenty-five minutes later, having awakened himself with a long shower, Frank was driving across the city, air conditioner blasting, navigating with his motel map. The Sunriser Café was on the inland side of Sarasota, away from the gulf, but the motif was nautical nonetheless, with a plank deck that ran around the outside, fashioned to look like a pier, and yacht club flags hanging limp in the grease-heavy air. Frank parked close to a wharf piling rising out of hot asphalt. He didn't want a lot of walking today; he had awakened with pain in his bad leg, and the shower had done little to ease it.

The Sunriser was set up with an open counter, above which hung fish netting and an array of plastic fish. Behind the counter a chef and his assistant handled the short orders. The place was busy with the breakfast crowd, elderly patrons mostly, with the chapped complexions that years of overexposure to sun brings. They didn't appear any more careful about their diet than they did about their skin, working on platters of eggs, home fries, and Canadian bacon. Perhaps they enjoyed the irony of the café's name, though probably they just liked the food.

Cruz was sitting in a booth halfway back, a pink paper napkin tucked into the front of his faded khaki uniform shirt. He paused from forking back food, and lifted a hand in greeting. Frank slid in opposite him.

"I can't drink bourbon anymore," Cruz declared. "It puts sponge inside my head. Probably why that bell was ringing so faint last night."

Frank was on guard; the cop's drinking had amounted to a few sips, which meant the mostly empty bottle was Frank's doing. "What bell was that?"

Cruz took his time chewing food. With his round eyeglasses and the napkin, he looked like a frog wearing a wide tie. A waitress cruised over on foam soles and poured coffee. "Chow?" Cruz asked Frank.

"What are you eating?"

"Catfish and grits with redeye gravy."

Frank's stomach rolled. "Just coffee. And some water."

When the waitress had gone, Cruz said, "Like this place? It always makes me feel young. Though it's a matter of time before we end up like most of them, huh? Pants up to our tits, the license tag that says No Phone, No Boss, No Money—only I don't know about you, I won't be driving any Cadillac. Or shooting twenty-handicap golf. Course, we could end up like your friend there, what's his name. Lou Lou Merloni?" The cool eyes behind the round glasses seemed to enjoy Frank's surprise. "Come on, Mr. Branco, did you think I wouldn't check at least one detail?"

"You went to Eventide?"

"I didn't get to talk to Merloni—he was sleeping—but I spoke with a nurse. Black woman with a Polack name."

"Barbara Wackowski."

"She vouched for you. Merloni gets pretty fuzzy in his head, apparently, so I don't know how much stock I'd want to put in what he says. But then, you'd know that. You were there two days running."

Frank's notion that the man was an efficient cop was confirmed. A little paranoid, perhaps; but that wasn't a bad quality in moderation. The question was, would Cruz have been curious enough to have gone into the pond? "What else did you learn, Sheriff?"

"Cruz is fine. How 'bout Raylynn Hazlitt?"

"Who's that?"

Cruz studied him a moment, then went back to shoveling in food. Frank would not have been surprised to see him eat black-eyed peas off a knife; but he had the feeling it was an act, aw shucks and pardon me all to hell, until the cuffs snapped shut and the jail door after them. The coffee came: hot and dark, and Frank sipped gratefully.

When Cruz finished chewing, he wiped his mouth on the pink napkin. "Patrolman Lee saw a baseball when she went into your bathroom to get that glass last night. A scummy old thing, she told me. Like it'd been underwater."

"It was. I found it in that pond."

"That's a long way from the ballpark."

"Lou Lou Merloni says that was a fishing hole for some of the Giants when New York used to play here."

Cruz nodded. "Find anything else?"

Frank had a moment's debate. Should he tell? Or lie? Or just evade? He said, "What's going on, Cruz? Am I being interrogated?"

From the seat next to him Cruz picked up a faded manila folder and took out a sheet of paper. "Raylynn Hazlitt," he said, squinting at the page from arm's length; evidently his glasses weren't bifocals. "She came east from Biloxi a couple years in a row. Worked a while at an orange grove the first year, and the next year as a waitress. Nineteen years old. A girlfriend reported her missing in April of nineteen fifty-seven. She was a 'Baseball Annie,' a camp follower. Liked to be around when the spring teams were here." Cruz set the paper aside. "I want to know what your angle is."

"With her? I never heard of her before now," Frank said.

"Don't be a smart mouth. You know what I mean."

"I'm interested in someone who was a major leaguer back then. He died recently in a car crash up north. Herb Frawley."

"That's the name you said last night."

"He was an outfielder for the Giants."

The cop's puffy eyes considered him coolly from behind the round lenses; then Cruz turned toward the short-order counter. "Hey, Jules. Play the name game for me. Herb Frawley?"

A bony black man in a white apron over a white T-shirt quit flipping pancakes and cupped a hand behind his ear. "One more time, Mr. Cruz?"

Cruz repeated Frawley's name.

"That one goes back a ways," the cook said. "Sure. He coulda been another Mel Ott—same kind of player. He still around?"

"He died recently," Frank said.

"Died." The cook moved a hand down over his apron. "I'm sorry to hear it."

Cruz said, "Jules is a fan. He knew Willie Mays. Didn't you, Jules?"

"Yes, sir. The 'Say Hey Kid.' "

"Jules remembers the days when some people around here

cried on account of the town lost the Giants. You can still catch the White Sox, or see the Pirates over to Bradenton, but it's not the same. Thank you, Jules. So talk to me, Branco," Cruz said in a lowered voice.

"We better get more coffee."

Frank told him about the flaming crash in Cooperstown, and of his own suspicions and investigation, including the blackmail note and the winding trail to Lou Lou Merloni. He said he was working for Frawley's former wife, though he did not mention Nola Dymmoch by name. And he didn't tell Cruz about the bat satchel in the bottom of the sinkhole, and maybe that was a mistake—Cruz wasn't a cop to trifle with; still, Frank needed to think carefully about his next step. He had already withheld information by not telling Cruz last night, so he was only compounding an existing sin. And there were worse sins for a private investigator. He wanted to speak with Gilchrist and with Nola—and possibly with an attorney.

Cruz said, "Are we talking crimes committed here in Sarasota County?"

"The investigation is still wide open. It's possible."

"What sort of crimes?"

"I don't know yet."

"They tie in with this young woman some way?"

"I don't know that either. I'd never heard of her before now. May I see that?"

Cruz eyed him a moment, nibbling a thin lip, then slid over the folder. Frank went through it. In addition to the sheet Cruz had read from, which was an investigation summary, there were two more pages. One was an old official missing-person report typed with a machine that had a combination red-and-black ribbon, both colors visible in the print. The date Raylynn Hazlitt had last been seen was listed as on or about April 5, 1957. The final sheet in the folder was the Hazlitt family's letter, handwritten in a looping scrawl and dated May 4 of the same year. In it they described their daughter Raylynn as being nineteen years old, five-

five, 124 pounds, "with a ample figure and good feachers and dark curley hair. A fine Godloving girl we hope she comes home to us real soon." It bore two scrawled signatures: her parents', presumably.

"She never turned up?" Frank asked.

"Not that I know of. That's from the cold case file."

"You wouldn't have a photograph?"

Cruz picked a tooth with the nail of his little finger. "Might could get one. Probably get dental records, too—the whole nine yards, if I figured there was good reason."

Cruz's implied question hung in the air as the waitress brought the check. Frank said, "I don't know. Frawley died in a car crash in Cooperstown during Hall of Fame weekend. There might be links to here."

"To that girl?"

Frank realized how tenuous everything had been, right from the start. He had been stitching meager scraps of fact together with guesses, working to convince himself and Gilchrist and Nola Dymmoch, and now this froglike little cop, that this was more than fantasy. And yet he knew what lay in the satchel out there on the bottom of that pond. That part was grimly real. "I don't have answers yet," he said.

Cruz plucked the napkin from his collar, wiped his hands, and laid it crumpled on the table. Motioning for Frank to wait, he took the check and went over to the cashier by the door, and then to the wall phone beyond. He talked with his back turned. Frank watched a tall old man in a pink seersucker blazer escort three attractive, well-preserved women out to a seafoam green Mark VII. Frank thought of Randolph and his flock of widows in Ocean Grove. There was an incentive to live long. Cruz came back and set down a dollar for a tip. "I open up case files to you," he said, "I've got an expectation of something in return."

Frank searched for and found no betrayal of information in the cop's face. He might have been a stone frog in a concrete pool. "If there's a link," Frank said, "maybe you get to stamp 'closed' on that file. I can't say anything more—mostly because I don't know any more. And I want to talk with my client. But if it makes sense then, I'll give you a full report."

Cruz put a toothpick in his mouth and didn't speak again until they were outside in the wilting heat. "I'll get this copied and see what I can do about a photograph, and get it to you," he said. "You limping?"

"I'm okay."

Cruz shaded his eyes to watch a pelican land on one of the fake wharf pilings, then turned back. "The case has been on ice a long time, I reckon it's not gonna get any colder over a few days."

"Nice images in this weather," Frank said.

"You've got my card. You learn anything important, you be in touch, Mr. Branco, you hear?"

"Branco's fine," Frank said.

Behind their lenses, the cop's eyes sparked briefly with what may have been mirth, then they were as flat and unrevealing as ever. "I'll surely expect it."

Back at the Gulf Breezes there was a message to call Gilchrist.

"What's up?" Frank asked when he'd placed the call.

"Willard Scott says Gulf Coast Florida is nice and muggy," Gilchrist greeted. "Hot too."

"Thanks for telling me."

"We got a storm coming. I'm sitting here twenty minutes waiting for a cab so I can take in some beer and food. I talked with the man in Cooperstown. Chief Bolick. Affirmative on Jack Livingstone being up there for both Sunday and Monday of induction weekend."

"Bolick's sure?"

"It's how Livingstone affords the good life these days. He's on the autograph circuit. Gonna be in New York City the next few days for a big annual card show. Thirty-five bucks every time he writes his name."

"Like signing checks," Frank said.

"Better. These don't bounce. Hey, cab's here. Later, man."

Frank called Eventide Senior Care Center and was told that Lou Lou Merloni's condition was stable. He was resting. No visitors allowed.

Frank drove over to the University of South Florida, on the Tamiami Trail, and located the library. They had seventy years' worth of the *Sarasota Herald-Tribune* on microfiche. Frank selected 1957. Knowing the preseason lasted from late February to early April, he made those the parameters of his first pass. The sports pages were full of the doings of the Giants, and the names came at him: Willie Mays, Bobby Thomson, Red Schoendienst, Hank Sauer. But clearly the big story that late winter and early spring was the two young sensations named Livingstone and Frawley, who spent the cool month of March chasing each other with hot bats. Livingstone had hit .384, while Frawley hit an impressive .388, with an .842 slugging percentage. On April 7, in the last game of the preseason, Frawley had edged Livingstone out by going four for four, including a home run, as the Giants beat the Phils. The papers carried no mention of Lou Lou Merloni, or of Raylynn Hazlitt of Biloxi. Bleary-eyed, Frank turned off the microfiche reader.

April 7 was the date of the old scorecard he had found in Herb Frawley's wallet the night Frawley died. Last game of spring training; two days after Raylynn Hazlitt was last seen. Three months later, Herb Frawley's career was in deep, irreversible trouble.

Sitting there in the cool summer-semester quiet of the university library, Frank felt a prickle of misgiving.

He got back to the hotel just before noon and the checkout time. A courier had delivered a large brown envelope with the Sarasota County seal on it. Inside was the photocopied material Cruz had promised, along with a small black-and-white snapshot. Frank drew it out. It was a posed, full shot of a shapely young woman in black hip-huggers and a striped short-sleeve top. She was leaning against a tree, one knee bent, bare foot pressed against the trunk. Her head was tipped slightly to the right as she looked at the camera. Sunlight threw leaf shadows on her face, but he could see the lush dark hair, white smile, the small, pert nose, across which he could imagine a spray of tiny freckles. There was a seductive innocence to the pose: a rural Annette Funicello waiting for Frankie Avalon to come by in his jalopy to take her for a ride. But whereas other teenage girls had had pictures of Elvis, Tab Hunter, and Sal Mineo on their bedroom walls, her particular attraction apparently had been for baseball players. Had it proven to be a fatal attraction?

He reread the reports Cruz had shown him that morning, returning to the letter from the Hazlitts, addressed to the Sarasota police, with its account of their "fine Godloving girl" with her "good feachers and dark curley hair." In spite of the misspellings and simple sentiments—or because of them, Frank thought—a poignancy came through, a bewildered sense of "why us?" That never changed, decade to decade, family to family. It was one of the sorrows police detectives had to grow inured to in order to do the job. He wondered if the Hazlitts were still alive. They'd be quite old now, if they were. He considered calling Biloxi and attempting to find out, but he decided it would be better to wait, to see if he could develop anything certain first. To rekindle pain for no reason would be cruel.

He packed his Patagonia bag. The old baseball was still slightly damp, so he wrapped it in tissue, put it in the wax paper wrap from a water glass, and stuffed it in his jacket pocket. The last thing he did was call the airport to inquire about afternoon flights to Boston. As the ticket agent read him the departure times, on an impulse, he changed his mind.

"What about to New York City?" he asked.

PART THREE

THE MENDOZA LINE

JACK LIVINGSTONE, 1956–1971

TEAM	GP	AB	H	HR	RBI	AVG	SB
1956 NY	151	574	202	31	88	.352	6
1957 NY	139	500	162	27	83	.324	6
1958 SF	142	539	156	24	94	.289	9
1959 SF	149	536	178	26	86	.332	14
1960 SF	154	585	191	36	103	.326	11
1961 SF	144	590	182	38	98	.308	10
1962 SF	82	303	87	14	54	.287	3
1963 SF	149	507	174	31	97	.343	9
1964 SF	159	541	158	28	92	.292	9
1965 SF	160	576	204	41	111	.354	7
1966 SF	157	550	199	43	121	.362	12
1967 SF	124	409	128	22	79	.313	6
1968 SF	133	452	122	16	76	.270	7
1969 SF	141	508	154	24	82	.303	3
1970 SF	123	418	121	20	71	.289	3
1971 SF	68	238	57	12	60	.239	1
16 YEARS	2175	7826	2475	433	1395	.316	116

Numbers on paper, but they represented so much more. On the
flight north Frank's mind extrapolated from statistics to plumb the

logic of human motivation. And what a motivation it was! For two decades, if you factored in his time in the minor leagues, Jack Livingstone had devoted himself to the task of being a great baseball player, putting up the kinds of totals that had given him immortality. But what did numbers and legend conceal?

If Livingstone was the ballplayer Raylynn Hazlitt had found herself drawn to, and something had happened—something terrible . . . And if Herb Frawley had found out . . . was that knowledge what had ruined his career? Had Herb been coming at Livingstone now with a blackmail try—pay or have your secret exposed? But *why* after all this time? More than thirty years. That part felt weak, illogical.

So try another fit. Suppose Herb Frawley's secret had been more than knowledge—had been guilt. Had he been party to some dark deed in that lost spring training of 1957?

Again, weak.

Frank slipped open the big envelope, took out the two photographs. The young woman posing under the tree, and the scrapbook photo taken at the Polo Grounds. He examined this second picture. Danny O'Connell, long gone. Herb Frawley, dead. Lou Lou Merloni—in a twilight of medication and memory now. Jack Livingstone. Handsome, smiling, unreadable Jack.

He looked at the snapshot of Raylynn Hazlitt, struck again by the dissonance between the frank flirtation in her pose and the innocence that shone in her face. If it was baseball players she was drawn to, he could see how Jack Livingstone would be a powerful pull. Somehow he was a key.

Merloni had called him a kink. Floyd Tillman had a vague recollection that it had been Jack who'd deflected Herb Frawley's attempt to rejoin the Giants. Why? Frank put the photographs away.

As the 727 came in across the New Jersey waterfront and the mouth of the Hudson, he looked down on the skeletal frameworks of bridges and piers, the herringbone lines of parking lots, the orderly grid of city streets. Pattern. The human need to superimpose order on chaos . . . And then, just when you decided you had it, a snake would slither across the calm surface of reason. The landing gear bumping into place jarred him. He shivered and got ready for landing.

With his Patagonia bag stored in a locker at La Guardia, and carrying the old baseball and the Sarasota Sheriff's Department file, he took a cab over to midtown Manhattan. The seventh annual Big Apple Baseball Card and Memorabilia Show was going on at the New York Hilton a few blocks south of Central Park. Signs in the lobby directed visitors past the ritzy concourse-level stores to the function rooms where the event was taking place. Frank paid the twenty-five-dollar entry fee and joined the crowds of youngsters and adults filing inside. Beyond the doors there were long tables with photographs and merchandise for sale to be signed by the players.

Time was rarely a friend to baseball heroes, Frank thought. Which was why books of nostalgia and these gatherings of the faithful kept happening: an effort to hold on to what could never really be saved. All those days in the heat of high summer aged the flesh, sapped the elasticity. Stop-and-go running took the spring out of the legs; and the erratic demands of almost continuous travel cooked off the vitality of youth, so that reunion days could be disheartening events, the equivalent of seeing the rock 'n' rollers of one's prime gimping about in TV concerts, singing in voices gone wistful and flat.

Frank looked into the first signing room. Sitting at tables in the front were half a dozen weathered men in sport coats, with thinning hair, some with gums gone bad from dipping snuff, each held apart from the masses by the momentary achievements of his youth. And if the time was a span of years, often the achievements themselves were far more fleeting: a perfect game in the World Series, a playoff series–extending ninth-inning home run, a spectacular leaping catch. . . .

Frank found Jack Livingstone in the second room, with Sandy Koufax, Jim Lonborg, and Dick Allen, each with his own table, and ushers guiding kids and adults into lines. Sitting there, his black hair threaded with gray, white silk sport coat darkening his California tan, Livingstone had kept his good looks about as well as Clark Gable once had. What was Livingstone now, close to sixty? Arrayed for sale and signature was a photo of him launching one up into the San Francisco Bay wind at Candlestick Park.

Frank got on the end of a line, which moved forward with efficient speed. When it was Frank's turn, Livingstone looked happy to discover that the crowd had dwindled for the moment. He let his smile sag and glanced at a gold watch on his thick wrist, the fingers of his free hand doing an impatient "gimme." He had made no eye contact yet. Maybe that cost extra, Frank thought.

"You got the photo, chief?" Livingstone said.

His voice was deep, gnarled at the edges like a well-worn fielder's glove. Frank slipped the dried baseball from his pocket and set it on the table. Against the spotless hotel linen, it looked like a shrunken head.

"How about signing that?"

Livingstone frowned at the ball but didn't reach for it. "Where'd you get that? Granny's attic?"

"Found it in a fishing hole in Florida. Maybe you could sign it right there on the sweet spot. Sign it, 'to Herb Frawley.' "

Livingstone's eyes came up slowly, narrowed and gray. His jaw lumped with some inner tension that looked dangerous. "What did you say?"

"He was your old teammate, no? Your roomie?"

Livingstone glanced past Frank and his manner softened. A young voice at Frank's back said, "Can you sign this picture 'to Pete,' Mr. Livingstone?"

Frank took the old baseball and stepped aside. A small, freckled girl was smiling through shiny braces. A corner of Livingstone's mouth twitched up in a stage smile. "Are you Pete?"

The girl blushed. "He's a boy I know."

Frank went out to the hotel lobby.

Ten minutes crawled by, and Frank was beginning to think that his approach hadn't been dramatic enough, that maybe he ought to have opened with the photograph of Raylynn Hazlitt, when Jack Livingstone appeared. He moved slowly, carrying a baseball bat. He spotted Frank and headed over, and Frank had the idea the man was going to attack him. But that was crazy. The lobby was full of people. Livingstone said, "I hit three-sixty-two with one of these one year." It was a simple statement, but was there a note of a threat in it too? The weathered Gable-face betrayed nothing.

"That was a long time ago," Frank said. "And you never quite reached Herb Frawley's spring training high of three-eighty-eight."

"What's this about, chief?"

"Come on, Jack. Try to guess."

Livingstone stared at Frank with tired eyes, as if this were just another outfield shift, one more effort to thwart his strength. His waist was thicker than in his playing days, but the shoulders pushing against the custom-sewn silk were impressively broad, and it wasn't hard to imagine he could still slug with power. "Who the hell are you?"

"It doesn't matter," Frank said quietly, conscious of the busy flow of people around them. "A ghost from yesteryear. Tell me, when did you see Herb last?"

"It's been years."

"You sure?"

"I said years."

"It wasn't a week ago in Cooperstown?"

Livingstone's eyes narrowed, crinkling with the lines from all those seasons of squinting into ballpark suns. He stared out with small gray stones. "If I had, I might've used this on the stupid bastard. Turns out I didn't need to. He's dead."

Not far away, several people were watching, probably having identified the Hall of Famer. They seemed to be planning an approach. Livingstone said, "Look, let's finish this in there."

The hotel bar was one of those skull grins of irony. The Sports Bar, it was called, with pennants, neon and darkness giving the recessed center the effect of a small stadium. TVs seemed to be everywhere, tuned to an array of channels: baseball, tennis, a surfing event. At this hour the clientele was mostly quiet people having quiet drinks. Livingstone staked out a corner, sitting with his back to the wall. When the drinks came, he plucked the cherry from his Manhattan, ate it, lifted the glass. "You've got till I finish this," he said. "Who are you?"

Frank told him, and showed his ID. Livingstone glanced at it. Either he knew why Frank was there, or he didn't care. In either case, he didn't ask. He chewed a few cocktail peanuts with slow deliberateness, then said, "I hadn't seen or heard from Herb in years, not since our playing days. Then, out of the blue I got a letter from him. Just a little short thing, no hello or anything. A threat. Said he was gonna blow my career out of the water if I didn't send him some money."

"How much did he want?" Frank asked.

"Twelve grand."

"Why that amount?"

Livingstone shrugged. "That's bird feed to today's players. Shit, the average salary is one-point-two million. Guys hitting two hundred, pitchers with ERAs of five, and some are getting that and more. My best-paid year—1970—I made a hundred seventy-five grand. Talk to Stan Musial, Ted Williams, see where the hell the game's gone." He jabbed at his drink, tossed the plastic stirrer aside, and drained the glass.

Frank had yet to taste his beer. "You sent it?"

"What?"

"You paid Frawley the twelve?"

Livingstone sighed. "I'm riding this nostalgia bus, and I've got some endorsements out on the Coast I do. Merchandise. I do okay. Yeah, I sent him the money."

"When was that?"

"Six or eight months back." He paused, perhaps to find some gauge. "Around New Year's."

The time matched the infusion of money into Frawley's Utica bank account. "What was his leverage on you?"

"Shit, that was a long time ago."

"Not long enough, apparently."

Jack Livingstone's eyes, which had softened—though maybe it was just the lounge lighting, or his private nostalgia—hardened again. He glared at Frank.

"He knew about you and the woman, didn't he," Frank said.

Livingstone stood up. "Screw you, pal," he said, and walked away.

It was a neat departure, no question about it. What did you do? Yell, "Stop in the name of the law!"? Call a cop? There really wasn't anything to do. So maybe it was time to get hold of Cruz, in Florida, and turn everything over to him. But give him what? Suspicions? Wiggy theories? Vintage baseball scorecards? Frank could see the old sheriff chewing on that for all of a minute before spitting it back in Frank's face like a catfish bone. No, what Frank didn't have, what he desperately needed, was concrete evidence.

He let his thoughts sink into the quiet background of conversation and television sports. By the time he'd finished his beer, he had an idea.

He walked out into the midday scurry along the Avenue of the Americas and went several blocks to Central Park. In no hurry, he went into the park and walked as far up as Seventy-second Street. On the west side of the lake, where a sign told him he was in the area known as Strawberry Fields, in honor of John Lennon, who had lived nearby, he headed back south. In the shaded corner by a large statue of someone named José Marti, he chose a bench facing the St. Moritz and sat. Very soon he would know whether or not his instincts were still working.

Five minutes later Jack Livingstone appeared. Instead of a baseball bat, he was carrying the note Frank had left with the hotel concierge: "Talk to me now and you won't see me again," and the place where he'd be.

"Thanks for coming," Frank said.

Livingstone glanced up at the statue, perhaps wondering, as Frank had, who José Marti was, and sat down. For a time he said nothing. At last he sighed, let his shoulders sag, as if holding up some old image had proved too burdensome. "Yeah," he said, "it's true. What you were getting at in there. But it took the two of us. She could've said no. Maybe I'd have stayed away."

He fell silent again. Frank waited. Cabs flitted by on Central Park South.

"There were always women around in those days," Livingstone resumed. "But she was something special . . . sophisticated. Beautiful. And those hot nights, with the smell of orange blossoms . . ." He leaned forward, his elbows on his knees, not looking at Frank. His voice had taken on a slower cadence, as if he were back among the citrus groves and moss-bearded live oaks of a Gulf Coast Florida evening. "It used to be like an itch. You're young and you've got this energy. You're working five, six hours a day, eight months a year, with your life parceled into innings, batting practice, road trips. Money comes each week, more than you can spend. But there's the rest of it, all this . . . time you've got to fill. So you do. You occupy yourself. Card games and drinking and golf. Like that. Fishing." Livingstone made a shrugging gesture with his hands, rolling the palms outward.

"What other things did you do?" Frank asked.

"Women were part of it too. You had . . . affairs. This one in particular, it went on for that spring-training season. It was crazy. I wish it never happened, on account of the way it turned out. I mean, how could a thing like that end good?" He turned to Frank for the first time. Was there supplication in the dark eyes? He looked away. "But you're not thinking about endings. There was only now, and that crazy itch you can never scratch. And then it did end."

"Just like that?" Frank said, amazed at the casualness, annoyed by it.

"Yeah."

"*You* ended it."

"I don't know who did."

"You mean somebody else was in on it?"

"I don't remember how it happened," Livingstone said doggedly.

Frank backed off a little. The man was talking, seemed to want to; don't scare him off. "When did Frawley find out?"

"Not right away. After. He must've been suspicious, but he never said a word. It was all there inside of him, I guess. Eating at him. He couldn't put it away."

"But you could."

"I had to. I felt bad, sure. But I had to stay on the game. Herb . . . couldn't." Livingstone was staring at his hands, still rugged and callused. Did signing autographs do that? Frank wondered.

"So after all this time, when Herb finally brought it up in that letter, threatening you, you paid him to forget it."

"He set the terms. I could've just told him to screw, tell his story if he wanted to. After all these years, you think it's going to matter? Who'll believe who? But then I figured, wait, how's that going to play with the kids?"

"Kids?"

"Fans, card collectors." He waved a hand toward the buildings and the bustle of traffic and walkers. "You saw them. In their eyes I'm still someone."

Someone who sold his name for thirty-five dollars a pop. Never mind the crime—*two* crimes, perhaps; it came down to a modern reality: in the absence of nobler models, pro athletes had become our heroes, and people wanted to bask in their reflected glory.

"So you paid him. Don't you know it's a mistake to pay a blackmailer?"

"You ever been blackmailed?"

"No."

"Yeah, well . . . I felt sorry for him too."

"Why? Because you'd also killed his career?"

"That's bullshit. *He* did that. He chose. I have my own reasons."

"I'd like to hear them."

"Why?"

"To understand."

Livingstone sat up. His glance was uneasy. "When the club moved west and Herb was finishing up with Detroit, he approached the Giants about giving him another shot. Management considered it, asked me what I thought about it. I'd liked Herb when we were here in the city. But I was having a good run out there. Those were my years. I'd found the groove. The idea of Herb hanging around, both of us knowing . . ." He shook his head. "It would've only jinxed us. I said no, and the front office went along. After that he went down to Mexico, and I never saw him again."

"After you paid him that first time," Frank said, "the twelve thousand—did he hit you up again?"

"No."

"He didn't threaten you? Ask for thirty-five thousand dollars?"

"No."

"You didn't arrange to meet him in Cooperstown?"

"I told you, I never heard from him again. And he never heard from me. And I haven't thought of any of this stuff either. Let it go, chief. It's long past."

Frank wondered if after all this time the urgency had gone out of the crime. Was there a point after which someone's death meant nothing? If Raylynn Hazlitt's parents were still alive, what would they say?

He watched a horse clop by, drawing a cab. The young lovers inside seemed oblivious of any world beyond their own. "You still remember her name?" Frank said with unexpected heat. "Or what she looked like?"

Livingstone turned. "What the hell do you think?"

Frank opened the big envelope, pulled out the photograph of Raylynn Hazlitt, and shoved it toward Livingstone.

Livingstone ignored it and stood abruptly. "Fuck," he said.

"Is that her?" Frank pressed.

"What's the point? What're you after?"

Frank stood too, adrenaline making his chest throb. "Damn it, Jack. I'm asking *you!*"

The force in his voice startled Livingstone. He stepped back, bumping the bench. "I've got an agent and attorneys. If this is some kind of cheap shakedown—" He glanced at the photograph. "If you think—" He blinked and took the picture. "Who's this?"

So, there wouldn't be any dramatic confession. That would have to wait for the criminal follow-up, if there was one. Frank would settle for some small confirmation, the quid pro quo for Sheriff Cruz. Cruz was welcome to the rest. In a quieter voice, Frank said, "I just want to hear you say a name, Jack."

"A name?" Livingstone rolled his heavy shoulders and handed back the photograph. "Yeah, why not? After all this time, what does it matter? But you got the wrong face to go with it, chief. It was Nola Frawley, okay? Satisfied? I was sleeping with the guy's wife."

22

DON'T THINK BADLY OF ME, FRANK. . . . I'VE GOT MY OWN sins to atone for.

The mind is a funny machine, surprising in what it will store for later use—or misuse. *I've got my own sins to atone for.* He remembered Nola saying it—not sure even when, only that she had. Was that what she had meant?

An unsolved killing—maybe two—the possibility of new evidence, a suspect, and Frank couldn't push past his sullen resentment that the woman he liked might have committed adultery thirty-five years ago. "Don't think badly of me," she had asked him, and he'd assured her he wouldn't. Until he had the chance. You shallow clown, Branco. You share a woman's bed for one night, and all at once she's answerable to you for her entire life? No, that was crazy thinking; but knowing it didn't make the fog in his brain lift, any more than aimlessly walking the city streets seemed to be doing.

Gilchrist's line was there in the memory banks too. *Make the blues your friend.* Da blues. It had become a mantra during the rehabilitation class at Boston City Hospital, Gilchrist investing it with as much pith as any aphorism in a twelve-step program. Though as wisdom it hadn't come any cheaper for Gilchrist than for anyone else: a superb athlete, who had used his abilities to soar, only to be brought down forever at age twenty-eight. There had been the dark time and months of rehab and regret and all the rest of it, but when Frank had first met him, Gilchrist was thirty-seven, a strong, self-respecting human being, doing good work. And he was flying again.

So okay, Frank wouldn't be depressed; he'd be rational. Livingstone could have been lying. Sure, why the hell not? He and Herb Frawley had been teammates, yes; but they'd also been rivals. Suppose he'd only *wanted* Nola Frawley. He'd had his pick of the little grandstand groupies drawn to his movie-star looks and big biceps—but his teammate's vital and comely wife: *that* would have been a prize. Except he couldn't get Nola Frawley, and so . . .

He stopped to wait for a traffic light. The red outline of the hand in the pedestrian signal seemed to say: "Whoa! Your logic is weak, Branco!"

Why would Livingstone lie now? What was the point? The rivalry had long since been decided. Jack Livingstone had ascended to the pantheon in Cooperstown, while Herb Frawley had spent his last sorry decade in a Utica rooming house drinking cheap beer.

The light changed and he walked on.

Make the blues your friend. Use them, like Robert Johnson had. And Bessie Smith, Howlin' Wolf, and Muddy Waters. Like Ty Gilchrist had.

When someone in the rehabilitation class had asked Gilchrist why, when he could have taken his insurance money and NFL pension and gone on the talk circuit or to Tahiti or anywhere, *why* he was there in the ratty dayroom at Boston City—the sardonic drift of the inquiry being that Gilchrist was just another dumb loser—Gilchrist had glowered like a rain cloud, and Frank felt a profound thankfulness that it was not he who had asked the question. Then came the radiant smile, the cloud vanished, and

Gilchrist told them he was there because *"some*body gotta save all you sorryass mothers from yourselves." Later Frank would come upon the Buddhist notion of bodhisattvas—beings who had achieved enlightenment but chose to forgo their entry into nirvana until all other living things became enlightened too. Frank knew the wait would be a long one.

So the current question became: Why had Nola omitted telling Frank about herself and Jack Livingstone? Because maybe Livingstone was right: it was a long time gone, when they were all young, and it had happened. And what did it have to do with anything now? Where did you go with that?

Frank finally went back to the Hilton. He checked the function rooms and the main ballroom, but the card show had wound up for the day. He found Livingstone in the bar. He was on a tall stool at a table by the wall, alone, and his body language said he wanted to stay that way. There had been more drinks: there was already a litter of cherry stems, like misplaced commas, on the cocktail napkin before him. Frank sat down across the table. Livingstone said nothing for a long moment, then made his gimme gesture. At first Frank thought it was a drunken macho invitation to throw a punch; then he decided Livingstone wanted the old baseball. Finally he grasped what the man actually meant.

In the dim light, Livingstone had to squint at the black-and-white snapshot: Raylynn Hazlitt leaning against the tree, smiling into sunlight at the camera.

"What is this," he said, glancing at Frank, "a paternity try?"

"Nothing like that."

He went back to studying the picture. "She looks vaguely familiar. What's her name?"

Frank told him.

"I remember her now. From New Orleans?"

"Biloxi."

"Got it. Raylynn. We used to call her the Biloxi Doxy. You want a drink?"

"No. Who's 'we'?"

Livingstone ignored the question. He signaled the waitress. In another dim reach of the bar, in Frank's line of sight, a weatherman was working a national map. He seemed excited, the way they got in New England in January when twenty inches was on the way. Livingstone said, "She worked real fast for a down-home girl—went with a lot of guys. She liked a party. You know, I've never been married. It wouldn't work. I've always liked women, but I can't ever seem to be friends with them. Friendship's not enough of a prize. I want to . . . possess them. And I've always wanted to go to bed with them."

"Who doesn't?" Frank said, not fully believing it, but wanting to get Livingstone focused again.

"Yeah. Anyway, I took her out. But I discovered a secret. I saw that under the wild image this one was really a settle-down type, and she was looking for permanent. She wanted claims on just one guy."

"What did you do?"

"I liked the kick."

"Kick?"

"The challenge. There were only a few weeks left of spring training, I decided, okay, I'll bring her around to my way of thinking. Life's a party."

"Sure."

Livingstone rolled his shoulders. "She was cute, and we had some laughs, but, man, she didn't get it. I'd tried to level with her, but she wanted to come up to New York and get domestic. By then we were getting ready to break training camp. Someone else volunteered to give her the word."

"What word?"

He shrugged. "That I was a no-good SOB. That I'd been putting the wood to a lot of chicks, and she was just one more. That I was gonna run out on her. Strong medicine, but that's the kind she needed. She wanted me."

Frank tried to push away an image of Livingstone with Nola. Who had ended that? "What happened?"

"It worked, I guess. I left, came back up here."

"Did you ever hear from her again?"

"Nope."

"Who was it who told her?"

Livingstone shook his head. "I honestly can't recollect."

"Herb Frawley?"

"No."

"You're sure."

"Not Frawley," Livingstone growled. "I can't—. Wait. Wait, yeah. Okay, I can see it. Now *there* was a snake."

"Who?"

"Weird, kinky. But he was cool too. He had his place."

"Who?" Frank repeated.

"This guy who used to get me things."

"Lou Lou Merloni?"

"I mean, okay, nowadays they've got the movies in every corner video store. There's even a line of X-rated bubble gum cards, which turn up at these sports card shows—but, hell, it's nude women. Big deal. Huh? No, not Lou Lou, this guy I'm telling you. On Forty-second Street. He'd come down to training camp with blue movies and whatnot. What was his name? He said he'd talk to this Biloxi chick, Raylynn." There was a silence, a sigh, then a chuckle. "The bad old days. Why, what's this about?"

Frank wished he had ordered a drink, to give himself something to grip. He felt himself twitching between anger, frustration, and a sour, growing conviction that Jack Livingstone was telling the truth. "That photograph comes from the Sarasota Sheriff's Department," he said. "From their cold case file."

"The cops?"

"Raylynn Hazlitt was reported missing sometime back around when you knew her. It's quite likely she's dead." He hesitated, then added, "Probably murdered."

Livingstone shook his head, as though trying to clear it, or to negate something wanting to lay hold of him. "Jesus, you think I had something to do with *that?*"

"Did you?"

"No. I mean, shit. I'm a respectable businessman. She was cute, I went around with her awhile. So did other guys. But, man, I didn't . . . " He puffed out a breath. "She never turned up?"

Frank was watching him intently, prospecting the weathered face for clues, for some trace of real regret. "Apparently not."

"God, man, I'm not into that. No way, no how. I mean, okay, I ditched her. I wasn't always cool. I was pretty goddamn insensitive, if you want to know the truth, but shit." Livingstone stood up so abruptly the tall stool rocked backward, grating on the tiles. The news had shaken him. He wobbled slightly, steadying himself on the table. "That was a long time ago. Is that what you're investigating?"

"Seems to be part of it," Frank said.

"Well, I don't know anything but what I told you."

"Who was it who got you the skin flicks?"

"I honest to God don't remember." Livingstone lifted the unfinished drink, appeared to think better of it, and set it down. "If you hear anything . . . " He let the thought go. "I've got an interview I'm supposed to do."

Frank said nothing.

"You know how journalists get if you keep them waiting." Livingstone gave a bitter smile. "I'm no zillion-dollar bonus baby. Can't be fashionably late."

Nor did he look either young or fashionable as he walked away; Frank could almost hear his joints creak. Remembering something, Frank pulled the shriveled baseball from his pocket. "Jack."

Livingstone caught it in a big palm, asking the question with his eyebrows.

"Nostalgia, Jack. Maybe you can get a few bucks for it."

By the time Frank got over to the high-rise apartment building on Twenty-seventh Street, the sky had begun to threaten rain, which was probably what the weatherman on the TV had been yammering about. Wind blew newspapers and grit along the sidewalk. Frank rang the bell and waited only a few seconds before Jason Frawley spoke on the intercom and buzzed him in. Frank took the elevator up to the fifth floor.

Jason was in a white shirt, the sleeves rolled in slipshod turns on his lean arms, his tie askew. Did he seem expectant, or was Frank projecting? Frank had begun to have a feeling of urgency, a sense of time getting away from him. He hoped he had conveyed that on the phone. "I dug out his things as soon as you hung up," Jason said. "It was there."

Frank had not said anything about Jack Livingstone and Jason's mother. He was pretty sure he wouldn't now either. He followed Jason into the other room. Herb Frawley's possessions were contained in three cardboard cartons arrayed on the floor. Mrs. Talarico, the landlady in Utica, had dutifully packed and sent everything to Jason. Two of the boxes had been unsealed and opened. Jason handed Frank a mailer envelope.

"This what you're looking for?"

Frank slid out the videocassette he had found in Frawley's room. *Lady with a Feather*. It had a copyright date eight years before. With it was a catalog from the company which had supplied the tape, an outfit called Black Satin Underground.

"You watch it?" Frank asked.

"Enough. What's the significance of it?"

"Where's the player?"

It was in the bedroom. Frank put the tape in. Together they watched the beginning, even less of it than Frank had viewed in Utica, and then he recognized one of the women. In the video she was a platinum blonde, but in a close-up of her face, which was supposed to show her ecstasy, Frank saw the unmistakable gap in her teeth. According to the tape box, she was either Candye Sweete or Dixie Harder, but he knew her in life as Lou Lou Merloni's brown-haired niece, Jane Syrk. He shut off the TV and VCR.

Jason Frawley was frowning deeply. "Well?"

"Can I use your phone?"

The number rang a long time and Frank was ready to hang up when a woman answered.

"Jane?"

"Who's calling please?"

Frank told her.

"Just a moment."

After a brief delay, Jane Syrk was on the line. "Frank? Is this about Uncle Lou?"

"How is he?"

"The same. I'm praying that God's will will be done. It's in his hands."

"I have to ask you something," Frank said.

"What is it?"

"That time we talked, in the pine grove—you told me about your past. What you used to do."

"Yes."

"How did that get started?"

There was a prolonged silence, and Frank thought he had lost her. Then, in a small voice she said, "Is this important, Frank?"

"It could be very important."

Another pause. "After I left home, I was living in New York City, thinking I had a future in dancing. That's because I thought I knew what was best, before I met the Lord. I'm a new person now, reborn. But I was lost then, blinded by the glitter of Babylon. Do you know what that's like?"

"I guess so."

"I met someone who had connections in theater, and we became friendly. He introduced me to some people, but mainly he introduced me to drugs. And then there were other people, all full of promises, and . . . the rest of it. The street life. Whoring."

"And the films?"

She didn't answer. Frank thought she was crying softly. "Jane . . . that's all behind you, and this isn't going anywhere but right here. I promise. But I need to know."

She sniffled, blew her nose. "Eventually that too, yes."

"Was there some person who got you started?"

She cleared her throat. "The same man. That's the thing that made me trust him in the first place."

"What was?"

"That he'd known Uncle Lou."

"What was his name?"

"I was on cocaine and then heroin that whole time, it's a blur, a terrible wasted blur of months and years. But you don't forget someone who does that to you. Who . . . degrades you that way. If he really did know my uncle, it had to have been long ago. And I never asked Uncle Lou—how could I, knowing what I'd become? He called himself Stephen North, but I know now he was someone else."

"Who else, Jane?"

"The tempter," she said. "He was Satan."

Outside the sky had a sickish yellow-green tint, like a poorly adjusted television set. The awnings of Indian and Pakistani restaurants along the block hung wilted and limp in the still, curry-spice air. Cabs were scarce, so he set out to walk. Jason Frawley had insisted it wasn't far. "You'll let me know what you find out," Jason had said at the elevator; and Frank promised he would. Jane Syrk had asked for no such promise.

As he made his way along the sidewalk, something came to him. He stopped and began to sift through the paper that collects in the pockets when one travels: ticket envelopes, tourist brochures, cocktail napkins, stubs. It was in his inside jacket pocket, where he had folded and stuck it that first day in Provincetown: the exhibit guide that Zoe had given him. He smoothed it open and scanned past names and dates, art trivia that meant nothing, searching for something else, which he hoped was there.

And it was.

23

FRANK MISSED THE ADDRESS THE FIRST TIME. HE WALKED right past it before realizing it was in an industrial building, a sooty, gray brick affair with fire escapes zigzagging down the five-story front. At street level, on Fourteenth near Third, there was a pizzeria, an ethnic grocery, and an all-male adult video arcade. The directory board in the shabby foyer confirmed what he knew. It also revealed that much of the building was loft space, occupied by studios, from something called Avanti Films to Zaitchik Sisters Ceramics. Black Satin Underground had a suite on the third floor. He pressed the buzzer.

You could go on pondering the odd nature of events all you wanted, call it synchronicity, coincidence, or chance that Lou Lou Merloni's niece turned up in a film found in Herb Frawley's apartment, made by someone called Stephen North, and distributed from this building; but in a city of eight million souls, it stretched the limit of belief that this same building also just happened to house the studio of painter Sten Nordgren.

He rang the buzzer again, and when there was no reply he tried Nordgren's studio on the top floor.

"Who is it?" a voice grated through a speaker.

"My name's Frank Branco." He hadn't thought of what he would do or say if he reached this point; it had happened too quickly. "I've got a message for Mr. Nordgren," he improvised.

Instantly he worried he had mousetrapped himself: the next response would request the message. It didn't come. There was a metallic click as the lock on the heavy inner door disengaged. Frank pulled open the door. At one end of a cramped black-and-white tile lobby stood an old cage-style elevator; Frank chose the stairs instead. The stairwell smelled of roach spray and stale cigarette smoke. He stopped on the second floor to peer into the hallway, which appeared minimally maintained. Some of the studios and businesses seemed active, but others looked closed or out of business. On three he found an anonymous black door, with Black Satin Underground indicated only by its suite number. The door had four locks. He listened at it a moment and, hearing nothing, climbed two more flights to the top floor.

In contrast with the lower floors, the corridor here was high ceilinged, with skylights and fresh-painted white walls. Most of it was occupied by the Sten Nordgren studio, he saw. Framed posters from gallery exhibits around the world formed an entryway to an open door at the end of the hall. Inside were two desks with telephones and potted plants, no one sitting at either. Ice blue fluorescent lights burned overhead. Something about the place struck Frank as familiar, but before he could identify it, a man in a striped work apron came through a back door, wiping his hands on a rag. He had a fringe of long dirty blond hair hanging around a bare, suntanned scalp.

"You the gent with the message?" he asked. He sounded British.

"Yes. Mr. Nordgren?"

"Not I. I work for the man. Tony Knight."

The accent was Australian, Frank decided. "Frank Branco." There was no handshake. "Actually it's less of a message, and more of a request," Frank improvised. "I recently saw some of his work at an exhibit. I found it very powerful." He thought of Zoe's treatise. "I'm interested in its relation to . . . abstract expressionism."

"You a collector?"

"Sometimes."

"Bum luck, mate. Nordgren's on the Cape right now. Went up this morning."

The news shook Frank. "Provincetown?"

"Yep. I'd try to help you myself, but I'm just a print techie. If you want to leave a number. . . ."

Now something else grabbed Frank's attention. It was a sign on the back wall of the workroom the man had just come from. Smoking Verboten! it warned in large red letters; and suddenly he knew what it was that had been familiar when he walked in. "What's that smell?" Frank asked.

Tony Knight sniffed. "I can't smell it anymore, but it'd be the solvent we use for cleaning up some of the resins we use. Carbon disulfide. Very nasty stuff."

"And flammable?" Frank said.

"Stuff burns like bloody hell."

By the time Frank got outside, it seemed as if the city had grown quieter. It hadn't, of course; people still scurried along the sidewalks, and cars and cabs swarmed the streets. Still, something was different, and what it was he realized was the light. The sky had gone an aquarium green. There was a breathless quality to the air, and pedestrians moved by with a rushed expectancy, as if by their own will they could allay what was coming. The neon signs in the all-male video shop seemed to sizzle as Frank went past.

He hiked several blocks before he found a phone booth, and when he slid the door closed, he was sweating. He got the number of the Hilton and called there and asked to speak with Jack Livingstone. As he waited, a taxi drew up and double-parked, luminous yellow in the odd light. An attractive, well-dressed woman about Nola Dymmoch's age got out, and Frank was aware that he wanted it to be Nola, wanted her with him here. The hotel operator came on and said Mr. Livingstone wasn't in his room.

"Could you check the card show, or the bar? It's important."

After a long delay, Livingstone grunted on the other end of the line. Frank identified himself and said, "What was the name of the man who supplied the porno films?"

"What? I thought we were done with this, chief."

"Not quite," Frank said.

"I don't remember that. You know how many years it's been?"

Frank said a name. There was silence, in the background of which faint cheering sounds told him the messenger had probably located Livingstone in the Sports Bar and patched the call through. As Livingstone's silence lengthened, Frank teetered on the edge of relief. He'd been pulling together odd lots and sizes, trying to make them fit, but they didn't. He'd been wrong and he was glad!

Then Livingstone said, "Where'd you dig *that* up? Jesus, yeah. Sten Nordgren." He was saying something else as Frank hung up the phone.

He tried to reach Nola, but a recorded message told him the long-distance lines were being checked for service and that he should try again later. He dialed Boston and got through.

"Where are you?" Gilchrist wanted to know. "I telephoned the Gulf Breezes and they said you'd booked."

"New York. Listen—"

"The card show? Did you see Livingstone?"

"Forget that for now. I tried to call Nola Dymmoch just now, but I can't get through. I'm going to give you her number, I want you to keep trying. If you reach her, tell her . . . tell her to stay put and wait for me."

"On the Cape? You going there?"

"I have to."

"Man, you better forget that noise. There's a storm coming. It's starting to get rough up here."

"Take this down." Frank gave Nola's phone number. When

Gilchrist had repeated it, Frank said, "Carbon disulfide."

"What?"

"The chemical I smelled in Frawley's car. It's a resin solvent, highly flammable. I've got to go."

"What about Livingstone?"

"Later. I'll call you from there."

When he hung up, there were long stabs of rain on the phone-booth glass.

24

THE RIDE TO LA GUARDIA WAS A CHORUS OF SLAPPING
windshield wipers and blaring horns. Rain had begun to fall in
earnest: big elongated drops beating the treed avenues of Queens
to a nickel sheen, and the humid air was spiced with smells from
the ethnic markets. All of that was just background, however, as
Frank grappled with other thoughts: like Sten Nordgren's being
linked to Nola's past. But it made sense she'd exhibit his paintings at the gallery, didn't it? After all, whatever he had been then,
he was an artist now. He had shows all over; his work sold. Art was
Nola's business. By the time the cab drew up in front of the terminal, Frank had gained a small measure of reassurance.

Inside, he retrieved his Patagonia from a locker and hurried
over to the busy concourse. There, flight-information monitors
were a blizzard of delays and cancellations as lines of irritable travelers inched toward harried airline clerks. The agent Frank finally
reached was holding on to her professional cheer, but it was being
nibbled away at the edges. Couldn't people look outside and *see*
what a crummy day for flying it was? She abused her computer key-
board awhile, shaking her head with each new data display. At last,

she said, "I'm sorry, sir. I can't get you to Cape Cod today."

"What about Boston?" Frank needed to reestablish some sense that he could still affect events. They seemed to be spinning beyond his reach.

The agent made a game try, but it was quickly apparent that Boston too was out. Service to Logan Airport had been cut back until further notice. Frank found a public phone not being used and called Nola Dymmoch's number again, but he got the same operator message as before. He called Gilchrist.

"I tried," his friend said. "But I haven't been able to get through to Provincetown. Big surprise. I've got the tube on, and this storm's looking rough, man. The Cape's getting hammered. So what now?"

"I'm going to see if I can get a cab to take me there."

Gilchrist didn't waste effort trying to talk him out of it this time. As Frank hung up and started away from the phone stall, someone said, "You going to Cape Cod?"

He turned to see a short, chiseled-featured man standing at one of the adjoining phones. He was straddling a thick briefcase and had the receiver to his ear, but he had clearly addressed Frank. "I overheard you mention the Cape. I'm flying there myself," said the man. "Hyannis. Tag along, if you like."

Frank had to smile. "You haven't got the bad news yet. The Cape is—"

The man held up a finger, cutting Frank off. He listened a moment, jotting information on a pad, then hung up. "Weather brief," he said simply. "Time to dee dee mao. You with me?"

The phrase struck Frank. It was Vietnamese, popular among GIs twenty-odd years ago. Clearly the man wasn't old enough to have been in that war, though there was a warrior toughness in his appearance.

"Do you know something I don't?" Frank asked.

The man grinned. He was muscular, in sport clothes and a black windbreaker. "I've got wings. I'm headed for the Cape for a job. Mark Doyle, by the way."

"Frank Branco."

Doyle's handshake was a vise grip. He picked up the briefcase and they started to walk. They headed away from the concourse into a branch corridor of the busy airport.

"Are you military?" Frank asked.

"Former. I'm a free bird now." Doyle explained that he was going over to do a job for Ocean Spray cranberries. The weather brief had reported a low-pressure area, part of the larger storm system, twenty miles east of Nantucket. "It's causing low ceilings and poor visibility, which is why the commercials aren't flying. But it's moving off." He knocked on one of the ubiquitous doors marked Authorized Personnel Only and they went through, into a room with Formica cabinets and a table. A uniformed security guard drinking coffee looked up. Doyle showed a laminated card. Frank didn't know what it was, but it worked. The guard got up and unlocked another door, and they emerged on the paved flight area. Rain was slanting in grayly off the Atlantic, puddling the concrete. The guard hollered something Frank didn't catch, and the door shut behind them.

They went past a ramp services area where a crew in yellow rain gear were brutalizing baggage from a commuter plane. The tarmac gleamed with kerosene rainbows, and the air was full of sound. "An old stick-mate of mine runs the FBO here," Doyle yelled over it.

"FBO?" Frank yelled back.

"Fixed base operation."

Frank could have turned that into a question too, but he let it alone. His shoes and the bottom of his pants were already wet. Shortly, Mark Doyle gripped his arm. "Right here."

If Frank was experiencing misgivings about having left the bright, dry terminal, the aircraft Doyle approached now gave him full pause. In the first place, it wasn't an airplane at all: it was a helicopter. Beneath its pale blue paint were the unmistakable lines and camouflage markings of a military helicopter of Vietnam vintage.

"It's a decommissioned Huey," Doyle called, anticipating his thoughts.

"Is this safe?"

"Safe?"

"In this weather."

"With me at the stick? Safer." Doyle laughed and pulled open a door. Somehow, the man's bravado was reassuring.

Inside, with the side doors closed, it was dry, at least, and some of the outside noise lessened. Once they were harnessed and helmeted, Doyle conversed with the control tower for a few moments. He looked unhappy when he signed off. "Worse than I thought. The storm knocked out power for the whole Cape, which means the radar at both Otis and Hyannis is out. I can't get any vectoring service. Instrument flight arrivals are canceled till further notice."

"When's that likely to be?"

"No time soon."

"Well, it was worth a try." Frank began to unfasten the harness.

"Whoa. I didn't say I'm not going."

Frank still had his hand on the harness buckle.

"I'm a small operator," Doyle said. "I've got this Huey—that yeah, saw action in Nam, if you're wondering—and I've got bills to pay. The ship's sound, and I can fly it. I can't afford to sit around waiting for the gods. Can't fly by radar? Okay, we'll file a visual flight rules plan."

" 'We'?"

Doyle grinned. "Whatever. I'll use dead reckoning. I'll stay down under the ceiling and scud run. It's all water between here and there anyhow, and with delayed arrivals on the Cape, there won't be a lot of air traffic to sweat. I'll be there in a couple hours. I. We. No pressure, and no charge. I'm going anyway. Frank, right? Your choice, Frank."

There was a directness about the man Frank liked, and along

with the bravado, it instilled confidence. But flying in a storm, without instruments . . . It seemed crazy.

It was already four o'clock. Frank's notion of trying to find a taxi willing to drive him to Provincetown came to mind again. Under ideal conditions, it was probably a six-hour haul; and the conditions were anything but ideal. Two hours, Doyle had said. He tried to envision other options. A gust of wind rocked the craft on its skids, and rain beat the windshield glass, and he thought of Nola out there with Sten Nordgren, unaware of what Nordgren really was. He cinched the seat harness tighter. "Does this run have an in-flight movie?" he said.

25

MARK DOYLE WAS ON THE PHONE FOR WHAT SEEMED LIKE a long time, much of it talking in acronyms that Frank gave up being curious about. He was figuring what he would do when he got to Hyannis, which was still most of an hour's drive from Provincetown, and he was without a car. During delays in the phone conversation, Doyle briefed Frank on overwater flight, door-eject procedures, and use of water wings in case they were forced to put down. Finally they were cleared for takeoff, and things speeded up. The chopper lifted into the rain, which was falling harder now, washing the world to gray.

"What's your line of work?" Doyle asked at one point, but before Frank could respond, Doyle was addressing the tower again, and the get-acquainted chatter ended. The craft roller-coastered on turbulent air for a time, seeming to move more slowly than Frank thought was possible, but soon the airport and the land became the same hammered-steel color of the ocean and were left behind.

A strobe light mounted somewhere atop the Huey flickered steadily off the encircling sheets of mist, and the dials and instrument gauges made a red mosaic before them, reassuring somehow in their steadiness, although Frank had no idea what they revealed. Except for occasional comments on what he was doing—defogging the windscreen, turning on the auxiliary fuel tank—Mark Doyle stayed intent on piloting, for which Frank was glad.

For his own part, Frank had begun to feel Aquarian. Rain hammered at the windshield, running off in streams, and he rode on alternating waves of near panic, swayed between the plunging flight of the chopper and thoughts of what might be happening on the other end of the trip, if he ever got there. There would be a calm space among the low clouds, or a conviction that Gilchrist had finally gotten through by telephone, and Nola was sitting quietly at home, drinking tea, safe, awaiting him. Then the aircraft would buck, drop into momentary weightlessness, and Doyle, tight-lipped at the controls, would scowl, and Frank's stomach would lurch all over again.

The world had been a uniform color of wet stone for some time when Doyle said, "There." For a moment Frank wasn't sure what he meant; then a red beacon pulsed faintly in the thick dusk. "Hyannis airport. We'll be on the ground in three minutes."

But it was closer to ten minutes before the skids dropped roughly on the soaked asphalt, and another fifteen by the time Frank was in a taxi taking him out the airport gate, turning north on Route 6. Frank had prevailed on Doyle to accept forty dollars for the trip. Probably, Frank suspected, just to get on his way, Doyle had taken it.

While landing had brought a measure of relief, Frank was nervous again, adrenalized for the last leg of a journey which had begun long hours and even longer miles ago in Florida. The bright heat seemed remote as a dream.

The taxi was a clunky station wagon, whose passenger seat had one of those beaded lumbar cushioners spread over it, meant to relax its occupant. Frank found himself shifting around, unable to get comfortable, his head full of rain thoughts. The driver wore a leather cowboy hat that drooped at the edges like his graying mustache, and the cab smelled of burned marijuana. He scanned the radio dial, finding mostly static with intermittent bursts of music or voices. He shut it off.

"I had tickets to the Sox tonight with Cleveland," the driver said. "Wanted to go out there and harass the Tribe, but I took a look at that sky this afternoon, and I said, uh-uh, no way's it gonna get played. Figure, that's what rain checks are for. What made it weird—around five o'clock we get this blast of lightning and thunder like an H-bomb going off. The power's out all the way to P-town, what I hear." He glanced at Frank, perhaps awaiting a response, or wondering if this information would make a difference in the destination. At Frank's silence, he shrugged; he got paid by the mile.

Rain blew in sheets across the highway. Frank fidgeted, the seat beads clicking under him, the lonely outer Cape landscape sliding past. Several times they passed light-and-power trucks, their yellow beacons flickering in the thick air; otherwise there was almost no traffic. Going past the high dunes, and onto Route 6-A through Truro, Frank had the impression of human habitation having been rained out, drowned, so it would be only a matter of time before all trace of it ran in diluvial streams into the Atlantic. He shifted forward impatiently, staring into the gloom, thinking hard about Nola.

It was nearing 8:30 when they drew into Provincetown. Gone was the familiar melee of street life. The Pilgrim Monument tower thrust into the low clouds like a Florentine dagger, oozing red in the gray sky with its beacon. The cabbie drove the maze of narrow roads in silence, stroking his bandito mustache and gazing out on what appeared to be a deserted village. Frank gave directions. On Commercial Street they slowed in front of the Dymmoch Gallery. It was closed, dark, as they passed. A sign in the window said, NEW WORK BY STEN NORDGREN.

"This way," Frank said.

Off in the direction of Race Point, there was a blink of lightning. Not for the first time Frank had the apprehension that his instincts had gone haywire, that the entire time, from Cooperstown to now, he had been missing connections, that truth lay far beyond his capacity to recognize it. And with this thought came a question: Was tonight, like that night in a Boston alley when Maximo Diaz had died, fated to end in tragedy?

"That's funny," the driver said.

Frank turned.

The driver craned another look past the rain-spattered side window. "Thought I seen a light flash out there."

Frank looked where the driver had been looking. For a fleeting moment he saw a shape visible across the land and water; then it was gone, eclipsed by a high dune, but he felt an icy certainty it was the big glass house that sat far out on the spit of land beyond the town. Nola's house. Dark as night.

The last part of the journey seemed to go on too long. They were at the very end of the Cape: How could it be so far? The taxi's lights made funnels in the driving rain. At last they made their way down the final strand toward the beach, and he saw the water for the first time. It was black and wind-driven, chopped with foam. Frank was trying to make out Nola's house in the gloom when the driver swore, and braked sharply. The cab hydroplaned a moment before shivering to a stop.

Through the fleeting clearness of the windshield, Frank saw the headlights on a large, moving puddle, then rain voided the view.

"Go through it," he ordered.

"The hell with that." The cabbie turned the wipers to their highest speed. "I swamp through there the motor's gonna crap the bed. I gotta get back to Hyannis."

"Go around."

The wipers banged faster, harder. "You crazy?"

"I'm paying you."

"That's no puddle, man. Look again. That's the Atlantic Ocean."

It couldn't be, Frank thought. But it was. The tide was high, and the storm was driving it higher, up across the low narrow land, moving to join itself on the bay side. Where it sat among the dunes beyond, Nola's house was cut off.

Frank paid the driver. He reached and lifted the Patagonia off the floor, glad for its water-resistant nylon. As he shoved the car door, the wind fought him a moment; then the door opened and he stepped into water over his shoe-tops. He swore.

The driver's response was snatched away by the wind. It sounded like, "Watch out for—" something. And then the station wagon's door slammed shut.

PART FOUR

HARDBALL

26

THE CAB WAITED A FEW FEET FROM THE EDGE OF THE rushing black water, its high beams dimmed by the relentless slanting rain, wipers beating a furious rhythm. Frank waved and stepped into the water. The unexpected force of the surge seized him, spun him sideways, nearly knocked him over. He caught himself, but in an instant the Patagonia was tugged from his hand. He made a snatch for it, but it tumbled slowly and went under. It was water-resistant, but not unsinkable. He stared at where it had been, trying to form an image of what it carried: clothing, shoes, the file on Raylynn Hazlitt. Gone. The current was sluicing the gravel bottom from under his shoes, threatening to take him too. He bent into the gusting wind and started forward. Once, he turned to look back. The cab was driving off, taking with it the last dry space in a dark landscape of water. Its taillights dissolved in the rain.

By squinting against the gusts, he could see the other side of the wash, maybe thirty feet away; yet still the seawater deepened. Unlike the night he had swum in it and made love with Nola, it was cold now, chilling him. It had reached his thighs, was rising toward his crotch when at last he felt the upward slope on the far side. He paused in a moment's exultation before slogging on.

He was soaked completely through when he reached Nola's big house. The windows revealed faint light coming from inside, in back, he thought, from the kitchen area. The glow was flickering, as if from candles, and this reassured him. He had an image of Nola in there, like the calm in the eye of the storm. Electrical power out, she had lit candles. In a minute he would be in her arms, and a few minutes after that they would be wrapped in the scratchy Navajo blanket, making love by candlelight, oblivious to storm and threat and the past. He banged on the door.

Beyond the porch, rain fell, black and bent in the wind. This was the only house out here, cut off now by its own moat, protected from harm, he hoped. The surrounding night was dark. No one came to the door.

He banged harder, tried the brass knob. Locked. He waited a moment longer; then, bracing himself, he stepped back into the storm. There was a car in the garage, an Oldsmobile or Buick. Nola's? He realized he didn't know, didn't know the simplest things about her, but it was clear to him that he *wanted* to, was hungry to learn all the small and private details and everyday cadences of her life. But where was she?

He started around the house toward the rear. As he went, he heard—or rather *felt*, for it seemed to come up from under him— a distant rumbling noise, rhythmic and powerful. But before he could identify it, it was eclipsed by a sound he knew: the high manic tinkling of the wind chimes on the back deck. He climbed the stairs to where he and Nola had stood four nights ago.

Beyond the glass slider, the kitchen was lit. He peered through, then tried the door. It wasn't locked. He drew it open, stepped in, slid it closed behind him. The light was coming from a hurricane oil lamp on the counter. He called Nola's name. No answer. Picking up the lamp, he began to explore the downstairs rooms. His shoes made puddles and wet sounds on the tile and wood floors.

The house was spacious and open, each room flowing into

others. For some reason he was struck by its contrast with the cramped little room where Herb Frawley had spent his days. The moving lamplight revealed antique and modern furnishings, big paintings, vases with flowers whose perfume spiced the cool rooms. Frawley's room had had its cheap furniture, the little Edward Hopper print, an aroma of decaying cheese. Odd where life's tides washed us, Frank thought. But there wasn't time to dwell on the past.

"Nola," he called again.

Nothing.

His shirt collar was a cold ring around the heated skin of his neck. As he moved through the huge living room toward the stairs to the upper floor, he stepped on something soft, which seemed to recoil from his foot, though the reaction might have been his own. It took him a moment to see the orange cat, waiting there by his feet, indistinct in the wavery lamplight. He murmured apology, reaching now to reassure it with a touch, actually said, "What's your name again?"

But of course the cat didn't answer; in fact, it hadn't moved. It was misshapen, somehow, and as he squatted near he saw why. The animal had been mutilated! It had no head!

Frank braced on a chair, his mind in momentary recoil. But his senses were alert. It was a smell that came to him, tingeing the edge of flower-scent, unmistakable. Then he saw its source. On the white wall directly ahead, someone had flung blood, thick splashes and dollops of it in a sick version of art, using the severed head as a brush—and the cat's name came to him. *Jackson Pollock*. Frank stared, his heart pounding. The senseless cruelty of the act enraged him, made him want to rush forward, yell.

He didn't move.

For a slow moment, he stood listening to the house, trying to sense what evil was here. Outside the chimes kept up a frantic ringing, and the wind groaned.

With cautious steps, he climbed to the upper floor and went to the bedroom. The big bed was neatly made, the fluffy flowered comforter in place. What was that? On one of the pillow shams lay a small stack of photographs. He set the hurricane lamp on the bedside table. The photos were black-and-white prints, about twenty in all. As he shuffled through them, he recognized what they were. They were crime and accident scene and autopsy photos, but not the official police variety. No, they were a private stash. Ambulance-chaser shots: people dead on nighttime streets and on barroom floors. Gunshot and car-wreck and suicide victims. The grim eye of the strobe lit details while the lens hungrily seized them: a T-shirt dark with blood, slacks and skirts stained where sphincters had let go, a glazed and staring eye, hair flung out in a graceful fan on a concrete floor, vacant corpses on stainless steel.

Why were they here? And the cat downstairs? Who had left them?

Then another photograph caught his eye. It was separate from the others, smaller, leaned against the face of the bedside table radio. It was a color Polaroid shot, still sticky as he picked it up.

He held it close to the hurricane lamp. It was of a young woman lying on a couch or low bed. A sheet had come partly away to reveal her nudity, pallid in the flash of the camera. There is nothing sexy about a corpse, not even if the person was beautiful in life, which Frank was convinced the woman was. But the picture held his attention for another reason, and slowly, like the first whisper of a rising wind, he knew why. In the slow dance of the lamp flame he could see the purple streak in the black hair, the pale cheeks. With a jolt of adrenaline, he recognized Nola's gallery assistant, Zoe.

He made a search of the other rooms, moving quickly because he knew he had to, yet braced at each moment for what he dreaded to find. But he didn't find it. The rooms were empty. If the Polaroid had been taken here in the house, the evidence was gone. The body wasn't here. He slipped the photo into his pocket.

He went back down to the kitchen and lifted the telephone. Dead. Big surprise. Far out in the gloom of the beach stood the wind-bent old shipwreckers shack, his attention drawn to it all at once because something caught his eye. The way something had caught the taxi driver's eye fifteen minutes ago? He stared but saw nothing more, yet he was convinced he had seen light flash through the cracks of a boarded window.

He stepped out onto the deck. Before he could react to protect it, the chimney of the lamp toppled and shattered on the deck. The flame gusted out. He put the useless lamp aside. His hands felt empty now, too empty. He wished he had a gun, but the hands themselves would have to do.

On the beach, Frank bent into the wind. The rain was turning the sand to a quagmire. It clung to his shoes, making progress slow. Behind him, the chimes kept up a continuous ringing which grew fainter, frailer, then faded altogether. He kept on walking. With the light gone, here among the rising dunes, it was as if older, more primitive currents rode the air. The hair at the back of his neck had risen like wet fur.

The shack was farther away than it appeared, and therefore was larger, the size of a cottage, he saw as he neared. He thought of Nola's story of Eugene O'Neill writing there, of ghosts—and the older story of criminals luring men and ships to their ruin with false lights. He reached the base of the dune, climbed over a tilted wind-fence, and started up through high grass. Beach roses tore at his wet pant legs. The shack was perched on the top of the sand, beyond which was a short downslope, and below that, he knew, a steep drop-off to the beach below. It was where he and Nola had swum and made love, but now, with the high, storm-driven tide, the waves sounded as if they were crashing directly below. That was the heavy rumbling he had felt. The old shack trembled with it.

The sand had sifted up over what had formerly been a porch, and creeper vines circled the tilted posts, their leaves clattering in the gusts. The front-facing windows were boarded. Frank pushed at the sagging door and it opened.

"Nola."

The only reply was the wind and the heavy spank of the surf.

Even with the door open to get what little outside light there was, the interior of the shack was impenetrably dim. He stepped in.

"It's Frank," he called.

He moved in farther, shuffling forward on the sandy floorboards, feeling his way with hands and feet. The place was a carpenter's nightmare: a *krazy kastle* of bad angles and oddly slanting planks. He kept his eyes wide, willing them to see in the darkness. His toe nudged something soft, and he bent to examine it. A pile of damp clothes. Then, as his eyes adjusted more, he made out the form of a mattress along the wall. He went nearer.

Someone was lying on the far side of it, curled against the wall. With his heart pounding, he knelt beside the mattress. There was a crash and he jumped. The wind had slammed the door shut.

He didn't go to open it. He leaned across the mattress and by feel discovered the person there was a woman. She didn't move. Her skin was cool. There was a rope around her neck, running down and encircling her hands, then looping around her waist. She was naked. Alive? He didn't know. He yanked off his sport jacket. It was damp right through to the lining, but it was warm with his body heat. He spread it over her. He started to loosen the rope. Could he carry her back to the house, find clothes, a blanket, maybe the keys to the car? He would get into town, get help.

As he began to rise, something crashed against his head. There was a burst of light that illuminated nothing, and he cried out a word. What?

"Hey?"

"Stop?"

"No?"

Just a word, which he forgot instantly, and he fell backward into a colder blackness.

HE WAS RUNNING IN SLOW MOTION ACROSS A FIELD OF
bright green grass, squinting to make out something in the lights.
The footing was soft and uncertain, more like sand than turf, and
the noise he had taken for an excited crowd seemed to be something else . . . a roar of wind perhaps, the pounding of waves, but
he couldn't be sure—nor could he concern himself with that. He
needed to concentrate, and that was making his head throb.

Something bit his foot. And again. A snake? He tried to reach
to pull off whatever it was, but he felt as if some weight were making his limbs heavy, impossible to lift, and he thought: I'm paralyzed.

"Come on," called a voice far, far away. "Wake it and shake
it."

He dragged his eyelids open over sandy eyes, once, twice. It
was an exhausting effort.

The light, he saw in fuzzy focus, came from a pair of hurricane
lanterns. The air was ribboned with their smoke and fumes, and
each flame was a bright dazzle that seemed to pulse with the ache
in his head. He lay on a bed, but when he tried to move he dis-

covered that his wrists and ankles were tied to the bedposts with nylon rope. He wore only his underpants.

Movement startled him, and a man edged into the lantern light. He was medium height, round bodied, with silvery hair combed back damply from a pronounced widow's peak. He was dressed in dark clothing: black pants and a black shirt that had a silken sheen so it appeared to shimmer in the lamplight.

"Who are you?" Frank demanded.

The man held up a short rod, tapered at one end and about a foot long. "Better than an alarm clock," he said. "Available in certain specialty shops. Reasonably safe." He jabbed the end against the bottom of Frank's foot. Frank yelped and jerked back from a battery-produced shock, but the cords holding his ankles and wrists restrained him.

"Damn it! Who are you?"

"Not only awake, but feisty too. Good." The man dropped the prod into a dark canvas bag on the foot of the bed. "I was worried there that our leading man would miss his debut. Weren't you, sweetheart?"

Following the man's glance, Frank squinted past the glow of the lamps into the shadows, and it was then that he saw Nola. She sat hunched on a chair by the wall in her white terry robe. He twisted, trying to face her. *"Are you all right?"*

Her hair, which had been wet, had dried in a wild spiky look, but her face was slack, her eyes darkly circled. "Hello, Frank," she said. There was an undercurrent of resignation in her voice he had never heard before.

"Has he hurt you?" Frank asked.

"Everything's cool," the man said. "We weren't planning for the power to go out, but we'll deal with it. Creates atmosphere. Like using this old ruin of a shack. Nola tell you the ghost story?"

"You're Sten Nordgren," Frank said.

"Well, shit, I'm famous."

Frank craned another look at Nola. She seemed dazed and out of it. Nordgren clapped his hands for attention. "I understand you're not crazy about my work, though," he said. "Not the way young Zoe is."

Zoe. He felt something like another small electric shock. Zoe was the person in the other room! All at once the full force of his predicament hit him as he realized the remoteness of this place. Plus the road was cut off by the storm. Nordgren had them in his power. "What have you done to her?"

Nordgren clicked his tongue. "So concerned for everyone. Well, you'll have your answers soon."

Frank struggled with the brutal possibilities, trying to think through the agony in his head, the raw burning in his wrists and ankles. He was pretty sure the man intended to kill them. Fear rolled in waves, like the heavy thrashing of the surf below.

Nordgren meanwhile had stripped a pillowcase from a pillow and busied himself tacking it to the plank wall at the foot of the bed. When he had it secure, he came back over, lifted some kind of machine from the floor, and set it on the mattress between Frank's spread legs. A projector, Frank saw, threaded with a small spool of film. Nordgren adjusted it and pressed a button. Evidently battery-powered, the device whirred to life. A square of light flickered onto the makeshift screen. Puzzled, Frank stared as black-and-white images appeared.

A dusty road. Water sparkling with sunlight. The picture jumped unsteadily. Sky. Water again. Pull back to reveal a pond. Trees. Abrupt cuts and a jittery camera. Then: a young woman . . . talking, though there was no sound.

"You'll have to overlook the production values," Nordgren said, trimming the wick of the lamp nearest the bed, dimming the room. "It was an inspiration of the moment, really, shot in eight-millimeter with an old spring-wound Keystone. The muse speaking unexpectedly."

A new shot. The same woman leaning against a car, something sporty from the 1950s. The camera panned erratically. Tropical-looking trees. Another scan of water. The day darker now. The car again, and Frank saw it was a Studebaker Golden Hawk.

Nordgren said, "Jack 'Love 'em and Leave 'em' Livingstone wanted quits with a girl who'd grown clingy. But he didn't have the balls to break it off himself. I volunteered to help. I spoke with Nola, whom I'd met through Jack, suggested *she* might have a chat with the woman. A girl chat. We took Nola's car and the three of us drove out to a pond, where I gather Jack had taken each of them before. Right, sweetheart?"

Frank wanted to glance at Nola, but the moving images held him frozen. On the screen there was another jump. A shot of an interior, blurry at first but coming slowly into focus. A paleness of bare skin. The image cleared more, and it was apparent the camera was shooting through a car window into a backseat at a man and a woman having sex.

The action went on. Entwined bodies: arms, legs, a back, buttocks. A zoom to faces in profile. The man, Frank was pretty sure, was Sten Nordgren, decades younger. But the woman . . . Frank struggled in vain to sit up higher; and then he quit trying. The woman's head lolled sideways, and he recognized her. She was the one in the snapshot Sheriff Cruz had given him. Raylynn Hazlitt.

Her eyes were closed. She looked as if she were asleep, or drugged. Her breasts jiggled as Nordgren tried to roll her over. She appeared to awaken slightly and resist, pushing at him. Nordgren hit her. The screen went dark for a moment, then the picture returned. Nordgren had his arm hooked around the woman's throat and he looked to be shouting, though the only sound was the projector's soft whir. A cold dread had settled into Frank's vitals, but he couldn't take his eyes off the screen, which was filled now with the image of Nordgren's arm tightening. Zoom to a close-up of the woman's face, mouth contorted; zoom to an extreme close-up of eyes, open now, staring. Staring. The shot went on and on. *Stop it!* Frank wanted to shout. *Cut!* He struggled to free one foot to kick the machine over . . . but that instant a question blasted into his brain, short-circuiting every objection. *Who was operating the camera?*

Nordgren shut off the projector. He lifted it and set it on the floor out of the way. When he straightened, his forehead was gleaming with sweat and his breathing had quickened. He turned up the lamp he had trimmed before.

"Raylynn Hazlitt," Frank said.

"We'd smoked some opium I'd gotten in Havana, and things turned a little *weird.*"

"That was her name. Raylynn Hazlitt, nineteen years old."

"Wouldn't you say, Nola? Weird?"

"From Biloxi, Mississippi."

"She was chasing Livingstone's ass. Wouldn't let go."

"She wanted to be in love with a ballplayer."

"Her neck broke. I didn't intend that. It just happened."

Just happened. "So you dismembered her and put her in a bag and sank it in the pond," Frank said, hearing the horror in his own voice.

Nordgren raised his brows; he seemed surprised too. "An athletic bag with Livingstone's name on it, in case Jack got too curious about where she'd gone. But he never did, never gave it a thought, I bet. I didn't really think about it either. You don't. You can't." His shoulders rose and fell inside the black shirt. "We went our separate ways next day. Back to our lives." He looked at Nola. "Back to Herb, for you, eh? Mr. Excitement."

Nola didn't respond. She was staring dully at nothing. The air was thick with the smell of lamp oil. Frank had no sense of how long he had been out before, or of what time it was now. He was aware of the muted surge of the ocean, or was that the rush of blood in his ears? Did anything outside this room exist? The entire world seemed composed of a narrow, choking darkness, and his own dread.

"That one little home movie," Nordgren said, "three minutes' worth—made everything else possible. I couldn't believe what some collectors were willing to pay for a print of film like that. Are *still* willing. Of course, the productions got slicker, the action better, sixteen-millimeter, sound, editing—shit, I even used scripts later, which was funny, hearing Mexican whores speaking words they didn't know. But I understand the appeal. Even with the most hard-core flick, the viewer's always aware that he's watching paid performers, and that knowledge diminishes the rush. But what if you knew that no director had ever yelled 'cut,' no fake blood was wiped away? That someone didn't get up afterward, put on her clothes, and walk off? Jesus, that's a turn-on. The ultimate cinema verité."

"Like painting with a severed cat's head?" Frank struggled again to rise, his heart drumming savagely in his chest, but the rope held. *"You're sick!"*

Nordgren stepped over and punched him, a short downward shot that broke Frank's lip. The taste of blood was immediate.

"Don't!" Nola cried.

"Shut up!" Nordgren whirled on her, his fist raised. After a moment, he lowered it, rubbing his knuckles. "Yeah, you're right. Let's just all stay loose. We've got things to do."

He picked up one of the lamps and positioned it nearer the bed; then he took Nola's hand and she stood up. He slid her robe off, dropped it to the floor. She wasn't bound, Frank saw. She wore a filmy nightgown, fastened in front with pink ribbons tied in bows. Nordgren led her over, and as she came, Frank could see her body under the thin fabric. There were several small bruises on one of her breasts. Nordgren settled her on the edge of the bed. Frank was aware of her rose-petal scent. When she only sat there unmoving, Nordgren swore. "Come on, get something started."

Gently she touched Frank's broken lip. "None of this was planned," she said, speaking slowly, as if drawing her words from a great distance. "I had hoped that with Herb's burial the past was out of reach forever. But maybe it never is."

From the black bag on the foot of the bed, Nordgren drew an aluminum tripod which he telescoped open and set up on the floor. Next he took out a small camcorder and connected it to the tripod mount. Nola said, "You came to me that day in the cemetery in Utica, and I thought maybe you'd discovered something. It turns out you hadn't, but when we spoke later and you had questions about Herb's death, I was genuinely surprised. Not so much so that I would've hired you, but I thought, if I say I'm not interested, will he be suspicious? So I did."

"That supposed to get the guy hot?" Nordgren sneered. "Christ, you'll put him to sleep." He took more things from his bag: sex toys, Frank saw—the kinds of things sold in porn shops. "Get something going. I'll get our ingenue." He picked up the other hurricane lamp and carried it into the front room.

With just the one lamp, Nola's face was halved by shadow. Her voice went on, unhurried. "At first I truly imagined you'd find nothing, and that would reassure me that Herb hadn't kept a diary, or anything incriminating. I believed the past is buried too deep ever to be found out. But then, that night when we . . . down there on the beach . . ." Nola threshed a hand into her thick, damp hair, lifting a shelf of it, staring into the dimness wonderingly. "That's when I began to believe that you could find the truth. It scared me, and yet part of me wanted you to. It was as if I finally had a reason to confront the shadow."

"Nola," Frank whispered, trying to fix her gaze, to pull her out of whatever fog she was in. "Untie me."

In the other room, Nordgren cursed. "She's dopier than I expected, but we don't have time. There're amyl nitrite poppers in the bag. Get them."

Frank looked toward the doorway. "Do what he says. Keep him occupied."

Nola's eyes flicked down to him, then away. Did she seem a little more alert? "Do it," he urged.

Nola bent to the canvas bag next to the bed and began to search in it.

"Is there a knife?" Frank whispered.

"Come on," Nordgren said impatiently. Nola drew out something and took it into the other room. When she returned, she fished in the bag once more and lifted something into the light. A hunting knife.

"My hands first," Frank said. "Keep talking."

She reached for the nylon cord on his right wrist and began to saw at it.

"I told Herb what had happened," she went on. "I had to. But what could he do? Tell the police his wife, the woman he had a child with, was a witness to a murder? Have his son grow up knowing that? What could *I* do?"

As Frank considered her questions, the cord parted. Eagerly he took the knife from her. His head was rushing with knowledge he had been after from that first evening in Cooperstown, and now he wasn't sure he wanted it. He could feel it filling his body, squeezing his heart. To shut it out, he began to saw at the cord on his other wrist.

"Damn you!" Nordgren cried in the other room. "Wake up, bitch." There was a slapping sound.

Nola rose quickly and Frank whispered, "Go in there, but stall him."

She glanced at him, nodded, and went into the other room.

Frank freed his left hand and his right ankle and was sawing furiously at the last rope when Nordgren appeared, backing through the door pulling the naked Zoe. Nola sent a panicked look at Frank. He wasn't ready—but time had nearly run out. He knew Nordgren intended to film and then kill them all, and this might be the only chance for any of them to survive. He slashed at the tough strands of nylon.

Too late. Nordgren saw him. With a shout, he pushed Zoe against Nola and charged the bed. He smashed a fist into Frank's face. The knife popped from Frank's grip, then Nordgren was on him, flailing at him with punches. Frank got a hand on the man's throat and shoved. As Nordgren toppled backward from the bed, Frank struggled with the ankle cord, trying to snap the frayed line. On hands and knees, Nordgren seized his bag and fumbled inside, pulling things from it: vibrators, short whips, leather masks, bungee cords.

"*Where the hell is it?*" he shouted, dumping the bag upside down. "*Nola!*"

The nylon cord had frayed nearly through, but still it held. Frank was straining to break it when Nordgren grabbed something from the spill of paraphernalia and swung it up. Pain exploded through Frank's stomach. He doubled over and rolled, and his weight snapped the cord.

Nordgren had his electric prod and jabbed again, hitting Frank in the leg this time. Frank dropped off the bed, hit the floor, and rolled. Cursing, Nordgren thrust the prod at him like a sword. It struck the bed frame in a spatter of sparks. Frank kicked at the man's face and Nordgren spun away, taking down the tripod and video camera as he fell. Shakily, Frank rose on the far side of the bed in time to see Nordgren rushing from the room.

Frank limped over to Nola and Zoe. Nola was holding the girl, wrapping her in the terry cloth robe. "She's alive," Nola said. "She'll be okay."

"I'll be back," he said.

"Wait—," she called after him, but he was going through the door.

Outside the rain had lessened. Squinting into it, he peered down the slope of dune, past the wind fence in the direction of Nola's house. He scanned the dark hills of sand, looking for the fleeing Nordgren, but there was no sign of him. Then, to his right, he noticed footprints in the wet sand. They went *up* the dune, past the shack. Why had Nordgren gone that way? Moving at a hobble, Frank followed.

The dune grasses reached to his knees, soaking his legs, slicing between his toes. Damp sand clung to his bare feet. His heart was beating at what seemed like dangerous speed. As he neared the back corner of the shack, he hesitated. Then he stepped around the corner.

Sten Nordgren was scrambling along the ridge of the dune. Beyond him there was only the steep drop-off, and the ocean below. Too late, Nordgren discovered his error. He stopped abruptly and looked down, and that gave Frank time to move. He had closed the distance to a couple yards when Nordgren turned.

He was startled. He raised the prod menacingly. "Get back!" he snarled. His breath came heavily. "You screwed up everything! You know that? Now you're fucking gonna die!"

He swung the electric prod.

Frank moved back, and Nordgren thrust again, stepping forward like a fencer. As Frank continued to dodge, their combined movement caused the lip of the dune to break away behind Nordgren. He looked back quickly and sidestepped to firmer sand. They were both panting, the thinning rain streaming over them. Frank rubbed water from his eyes. "It's over," he said.

"Only for you!" Nordgren lunged.

Frank had to jump sideways to avoid the prod, and as he did the entire bank quivered. Nordgren felt it too. He glanced down to see the dune shudder and begin to crumble. He hurled the prod at Frank. He tried to run, but the wet sand was caving in too quickly. He lost his balance. Frank made a grab for him, but with nothing firm to shove off from he only sprawled headlong. Nordgren started to pinwheel his arms and seemed to shorten and shrink, and then the bank broke away completely.

Nordgren, his black shirt flapping in the wind, went down with a long, shrill scream.

Frank scrambled back from the still-collapsing dune. When it stopped, he edged forward. Beyond the broken ridge of sand he could see the surf, forty feet below. He scanned the water, looking for Nordgren, half-certain the man would somehow get ashore. But the beach was gone completely in a mad white swirl. Then he saw him. Nordgren was being dragged seaward by the undertow, his silver hair spiked up like a wild crown, his mouth stretched wide in a silent scream. A wave broke over him and he went under for a moment, then came up, one arm thrust above the surge, hand clenched in a fury of demand. Unsteadily, keeping his eyes on the man, Frank got to his feet. Again Nordgren went underwater, and again rose, raging like an impotent sea king. Frank watched.

28

When Frank got back inside the shack, the air was smoky with the guttering oil lamps. Nola had managed to get Zoe onto the bed and covered her with the white robe.

"How is she?"

"She'll be all right."

"Good."

"Did Sten—"

"Gone. Drowned, I think."

For a moment Nola's eyes held his, pained and probing in the dance of shadow and light; then she nodded and went back to tending Zoe. Frank found his clothes nearby and drew them on. As he tied his shoes, he thought that if he could just pull Nola against him, hold her close, some of this madness would disappear. The rest . . . maybe he could learn to live with the rest. . . .

When he looked up, Nola had gone.

He found her standing atop the broken dune, gazing out to sea. For a moment he thought she was searching for Sten Nordgren; then he saw she was looking at the sky, where the low clouds were moving fast, beginning to break up.

"It's over now," he said to her back.

She nodded.

"Why don't we get Zoe and go back to your house. We should get the police."

When Nola turned he saw the gun. It was a small nickel-plated automatic, and he realized it was what Nordgren had been looking for earlier. Nola had found it. Was it aimed at him? The wind pasted the thin nightgown to her body. "We ought to go inside," he said again.

"There isn't anything to say."

"All right," he agreed. "We can talk later."

"I feel bad about having involved you, Frank." She took a couple steps toward the shack, then turned again. "And having lied to you."

When? he wondered. From the very first day they had talked? On their night together? Ever since? He said, "My experience is that people in trouble almost always do. It's pretty natural." Was he offering her some other way, or was it for himself, a sop to his ego? "I would imagine that after that time at the pond, you were vulnerable. Nordgren had power over you. You're not the only one."

Nola pushed her hair back, still pointing the gun. "At first he was just a dealer in dirty books. Jack and some of the other players liked it. Never Herb, though. Straight-arrow Herb. God, I wish we could undo things we've done, make up to the people we've hurt." She pushed back her windblown hair. "On his own, Sten started making skin flicks with prostitutes. But his big discovery came by chance, that evening in Florida."

Frank swallowed. "There's time for this later. You must be cold."

"I think he meant only to frighten the girl, use the film as leverage in case she kept pursuing Jack. But it got too rough. Something happened. I didn't realize it at first, so I kept filming. He said to. Then I knew. I was badly shaken. Hysterical nearly. But he stayed so calm. He put her in the woods, dropped me off in Palmetto, then went back out and took care of . . . everything. We didn't see each other after that. Much later I found out he'd made prints of the film and sold them for a lot of money. I never knew what happened to the girl's body until tonight. You found it?"

His stomach was twisted tight. "I think so."

She nodded.

"Nordgren mentioned other films. . . ."

"I'm not sure. There was the incident in Mexico."

"When Herb was playing ball there?"

Nola shook her head ruefully. "You really are some kind of detective. Yeah, when Herb's plan for a comeback didn't work out, someone suggested he try Mexico."

The someone was Lou Lou Merloni, Frank realized. In his mind he could hear the old man's raspy voice telling it, his meeting Herb at Alligator Al's. Merloni had even recommended a place where Frawley might stay. The fixer and the pornographer. They'd known each other through old links—enough, Frank saw now, so that years later, Nordgren could trade on that to befriend Lou Lou's niece, Jane, and use her.

"Herb ended up staying in Sten's villa there. One night . . ." Nola drew a steadying breath. "This is all secondhand, told to me much later."

"Nola, you don't have to—"

"One night Herb came home drunk—common enough by then—and he walked into the wrong room, right into the middle of . . . something bad."

Frank felt a quiver of fear, even glanced around with the odd sensation that Nordgren has somehow escaped the surf, was creeping toward them. Crazy. He shifted his stance, wanting to ease the ache in his bad leg. "Nordgren was making snuff films there?"

"Whatever he was up to, it spooked Herb. He got violently ill. He was taken to a hospital with alcohol poisoning, the d.t.'s. When he finally left Mexico, baseball was out for good. He was broken. Sten just . . . prospered. Years later he used his leverage on me so I'd get my second husband to exhibit his painting. Eventually, when the work built its own following, I'd somehow managed to put all that past aside. Sten actually was a very gifted painter."

As if that mattered, Frank thought, and discovered in himself a new disappointment in Nola. He pushed it away, needing only clarity now. "You knew nothing about Cooperstown?"

"No."

"Seven months ago Herb blackmailed Jack Livingstone for twelve thousand dollars. He used the fact that you and Jack . . . that you'd . . ." He let it go. "Then, recently Herb made a connection between Nordgren and a porno operation in New York called Black Satin Underground. I think he tried to shake down Nordgren. He planned to give the money to Jason."

"To Jason?"

"Apparently Herb wanted reconciliation too."

She considered that a moment. "I had no idea. About any of that. It sounds like a dumb plan."

"Nordgren must've arranged to meet Herb in Cooperstown, killed him, and staged the car crash. He intended the past to burn up in that wreck."

"But you were there," Nola said, her voice quiet in the lessening wind. "And here tonight too. Mr. Detective. I thank you."

With the nightgown pasted to her, she seemed girl-like again. He wanted to go to her, put his arms around her. But she had the gun.

"You've convinced me of a lot of things, Frank. Things I'd forgotten and moved beyond, I thought. Feelings, even. Since that night down there on the beach, I've been like a girl again. Can you believe it? At my age?" He was close enough to see the weak smile she offered—almost close enough to take the gun. "Except that shadow side. Old Carl Jung. God, it doesn't go away, does it. Maybe I could make others believe it was fear that kept me silent all these years. Fear, and victimhood. And I swear, I never dreamed things would turn out like they did in Florida. I've been haunted by that girl ever since. Taking Zoe in, treating her as my daughter, has been a kind of penance. But I don't think I can convince myself any longer that I'm blameless. I wasn't then—I'd cheated on Herb with Jack Livingstone, partly because Herb was just so *straight*. I wanted excitement, kicks. And I'm sure as hell not blameless now."

"Nola, why don't we—"

"No. Listen to me. You have to understand this. *I* have to. When Sten came to the gallery this afternoon—obviously with some of this planned—I was expecting an art exhibit. Zoe was so thrilled to meet him. Then the power went out, and we had to come back to my house . . . and . . ." She shut her eyes and shook her head. "He had that terrible bag with him. With drugs and rope and . . ." She moved the gun. "This too. He gave Zoe an injection of something. When I tried to stop him, he hit me. He was ready to . . . despoil her."

Like he had Raylynn Hazlitt, Frank thought, and Jane Syrk; perhaps young Nola Frawley even.

"I told him about your investigation, hoping it would scare him off. It only pushed him all the way to the limit. He'd have killed her, Frank, and you too." Her voice strained with inner anguish, just audible over the rumble of waves. "Now I feel like I've peered over a brink and seen that I'm as corrupted as he was. Can you understand that, how that could happen to someone?"

He was trying, struggling to find a way into her vision; but before he could speak, Nola shook her head. "No, you can't." And before he could contradict her or get nearer, she asked, "What was her name again?"

"Raylynn."

Nola nodded. Holding the gun aimed at his chest, she looked up. "No stars tonight."

He looked up too, aware as he did that it was a mistake; and in that instant she was past him. He felt her motion, heard the churn of wet sand beneath her feet. He lunged, getting hold of the sheer nightgown, which tore away in his hand, and she went over the edge.

She never cried out.

*　*　*

Frank didn't know how long he gazed down from the shattered dune, searching the waves for some human motion. The rain had mostly stopped and the wind was dying. The storm was escaping out to sea, just as Mark Doyle's weather briefing had said it would; but there was still a high tide, and the surf pounded the shore relentlessly. After another few minutes he gave up. He held the torn nightgown to his face a moment, breathed the lingering scent of roses, then lifted the thin garment to the wind and it was gone.

Zoe lay on the bed, paler than usual, drawn into a fetal curl under the terry robe. She stirred when he wrapped a blanket around her, and moaned as he picked her up. Speaking to her in a calming voice he wasn't sure she heard, he carried her outside and started back across the empty dunes. He had no idea what time it was. He only knew he desperately wanted to sleep. It took a long time to reach the house.

EPILOGUE

"WHAT?"

"Denzell Deplain," Gilchrist repeated with exaggerated patience.

"The guy who blind-sided you. Yeah. So?"

"That's what I'm telling you. He never apologized."

"I know. He even bragged in his book about how hard he was. The idiot."

"Wait. Then I ran into him one time at a banquet. I ever told you this?"

"No."

"I don't like to repeat myself."

"I'm listening. No, you never told me."

They were in Gilchrist's South End apartment. The TV played soundlessly across the room: a late season game, the Sox and the Yankees. "Denzell was still quick. Knocked over chairs trying to sneak out the back. Only thing, the doors were locked. So I corner him with my chair. Motor right in so my wheels are practically parked on top of his Guccis, and his Super Bowl ring is a foot from my face. Got the picture?"

"I think so."

"He had to deal with me."

"Who doesn't? What did you do?"

"I made this sign in the air—" Gilchrist did it now: up and down, back and forth. "And I said, 'Bless you, my child.' "

"Bless you."

"Or words to that effect."

Frank frowned. "And?"

"I smiled at him."

"What did Deplain do?"

"You're missing the point."

"Wait. You corner the guy who paralyzed you, and his reaction isn't the point?"

"Not the point I'm getting at here."

Frank sighed, let his eyes flick to the TV screen. The Yankees manager was signaling the bullpen for a left-hander. Frank looked back at Gilchrist. "Okay, I'll bite."

"Come on, man, have I got to do everything for you?"

"Message being maybe . . . what he did isn't important. Point is . . . go easy on yourself? And others?"

"Or words to that effect." Gilchrist rolled over nearer the TV. "I love it," he said. "With the bottom of the order coming up they're closing with a southpaw?"

But Frank wasn't interested. It was as if, for the first time, the hollowness of his life had been laid bare to his eyes. So empty of meaning was it that he had become a watcher of other people's staged dramas. He couldn't be bothered. He had his own to deal with. For days a question had been going around in his mind: How witting had Nola Dymmoch been in all that had happened?

After getting Zoe back to the big house, he had revived her, gotten her dressed, carried her to the car there under the carport, and driven her to the Provincetown police station. He had provided only necessary information, and they put her into an ambulance and took her to the hospital in Hyannis. Then Frank sat with the police and gave them more. He accompanied them out to Nola's house and the old shipwreckers shack on the dunes. When the detectives rewound the eight-millimeter film and started the projector, Frank stepped outside to breathe the ocean air.

Nola's body had been recovered from the surf. No trace was found of Sten Nordgren; not surprising, the cops said, when you considered the currents off Race Point. Given Nola's position in the community, the police were understandably interested in keeping their investigation quiet at first, and understandably skeptical of Frank's status with regard to it. There were communiques with the Boston Police, who confirmed Frank's former employment there and vouched for his current status. Eventually the case became news, with jurisdictions in Florida and New York state getting involved. Frank had to deal again, via telephone, with Chief James R. Bolick in Cooperstown, and Cruz, in Sarasota County, both of whom were appreciative. He also called Jane Syrk and gave her an account of events. She sounded genuinely sorry for everyone. She was, however, happy to report that her uncle Lou was on his feet again and "full of the devil"—laughing as she said it.

Jason Frawley came up for the funeral of his mother. Nola was buried in a small Cape Cod cemetery, in a plot next to the man who'd had the foresight to buy Jackson Pollocks before they became expensive. Of the cat named for the painter, Frank had no final word, though he had asked that after the crime scene was photographed and evidence taken, the cat be buried in the dunes behind Nola's house. He never found out if this was done.

To the investigators Frank revealed nothing beyond what appeared to be the facts of the case: that Nordgren, artist and pornographer, had come for an opening of his show, and had attacked both women during the storm. The dark-haired woman in the old film was identified as Raylynn Hazlitt, and dental records confirmed that the skeletal remains found in the bag in Florida were hers. The film showed Nordgren as her killer. Frank said he had no idea who had operated the camera. He decided to let it all fall on Nordgren.

Cruz called back to say Raylynn Hazlitt's parents were deceased, but some cousins still living in Mississippi had been told of her death. They said something about the satisfaction of know-ing. As for Frank's own satisfaction in knowing . . .

Gilchrist turned from a commercial for Japanese trucks. He gave Frank a glance, then shut off the TV with the remote. He said, "There are caves in Central America where they have these fish who've been living there so many generations they've evolved to sightlessness. They're born without eyes."

"Yeah?" Frank said listlessly.

"I've been thinking, it's probably a lot less hassle to be born without eyes than it is to lose them. Or legs, too, I imagine. But sometimes it's nice to remember what it was to have seen. Or run. Or . . ." He let it lie.

"Go ahead, Zen me out," Frank said. "I'm a sitting duck."

On a late September afternoon, when the Sox had a make-or-break game for play-off contention, Frank and Gilchrist made their way along Lansdowne Street toward Fenway Park. The air was full of sunshine and the cries of souvenir hawkers and food vendors. That morning Frank had received a post card from Zoe inviting them to the opening of a new exhibit: watercolor still lifes by a grand-mother from the English lakes district. He had called Zoe to share the laugh, and before she hung up she quietly admitted to having slashed and burned all of the Nordgren materials.

"Gee, what a loss," Gilchrist said when Frank told him. "I won-der if lawyers will show up sometime with paper in hand, asking about the paintings?"

"What paintings?"

"Yeah."

With some frequency these days, Frank would catch himself thinking of that August night in the surf, with the sea sparkling around him and Nola Dymmoch. However much more he wished there could have been, he had that. Was he was finally starting to learn about making the blues a friend?

When the National Anthem began, Frank noticed a young

guy in the row in front of them deliberately not standing. It irked him, and he was considering spilling a beer on the guy's head when Gilchrist leaned close to the man's ear and said something Frank couldn't hear. The man turned slightly, then stood at once.

Later, as they left the park in the knowledge that for the seventy-seventh consecutive season no World Championship would come home to Boston, Gilchrist asked, "Why do we do it?"

"Baseball?"

"That'll do for now, unless you want to go metaphysical."

"No. Though I would like to know what you said to that kid during the anthem."

"I told him I'd change places with him anytime, asked if he wanted my seat."

"Buddha strikes again."

"Don't evade the question."

"About why we do it?"

"Year after year, spend our money, get our hearts stomped on, get kicked in the teeth."

"I don't know."

"No?"

"Is this a quiz?"

But Gilchrist did not answer, stayed quiet all the way to Kenmore Square, and into a little rathskeller where the beer was cold. And finally Frank said, "Because we're fans."

Gilchrist grinned and held out his palm for Frank to slap. "Welcome back."